A Fantasy Medley 3

A Fantasy Medley 3

Edited by Yanni Kuznia

Subterranean Press 2015

First Edition

ISBN
978-1-59606-767-7

Subterranean Press
PO Box 190106
Burton, MI 48519

subterraneanpress.com

For Brianna, Calista, and Deirdre:
my sun, my moon, and my star

Table of Contents

Goddess at the Crossroads

KEVIN HEARNE

Author's note: In the Iron Druid Chronicles chronology, this story takes place during Granuaile's training period, after Tricked *but before the novella* Two Ravens and One Crow.

There is no industrial hum under the skies of the Navajo Nation, and the stars float bright and naked in them, unveiled by the urban gauze of pollution. And in that clarity all you hear is the song the earth decides to sing—well, that, and whatever noise you make yourself. The crackle and whoosh of wood as it burns under a bubbling stewpot is some of my favorite music, and visually it can be mesmerizing—and evocative.

"Fire burn and cauldron bubble," Granuaile intoned, staring into the orange heart of the blaze of our campfire as she quoted the witches from Shakespeare. The words triggered a memory and I shivered involuntarily. My apprentice caught it, looking up from the fire. "What? Are you spooked by those fictional hags?"

"Not the fictional ones, no," I said, and Granuaile grew still, staring at me. Oberon, my Irish Wolfhound, was curled up outside the ring of hearthstones and sensed that some tension had crept too close to the fire. He raised his head and spoke to me through our mental bond.

<Atticus? What's going on?>

Granuaile wasn't bound to the earth yet and she couldn't hear Oberon, but she had learned to pick up some of his cues. "If Oberon's asking you what's up, I'd like to know too. What made you shudder like that?"

I briefly wondered if I should tell her or dodge the question, but then remembered she had already seen plenty of things she'd never unsee through her association with me. The visage of Hel, for example, Norse goddess of the dead, was nightmare fuel enough for any lifetime, and she hadn't cracked yet.

"It's a bit of a story, but I suppose we have the time for it."

"We absolutely do," Granuaile agreed. "We have a fire, honest-to-goodness stew that's been cooking all day, and some beers in the cooler. And no chance of being interrupted." She waggled a finger at me. "That's key."

"Indeed. Well, it's a story from England shortly after the death of Queen Elizabeth, when Shakespeare had a new patron in Scottish Jimmy—"

"Scottish Jimmy?"

"That was what the irreverent called King James back then. That was the politest term, actually."

"We're talking about the namesake of the King James Bible?"

"Precisely."

"Hold on. I know you have all of Shakespeare's works memorized, but did you actually meet him?"

"Not only did I meet him, I saved his life."

Granuaile gaped. She knew that my long life had acquainted me with a few celebrated historical figures but I could still surprise her. "How have you not told me this before?"

Shrugging, I said, "There was always a chance we'd be interrupted before, and as you said, that's key. And I didn't want to be a name-dropper."

"So is saving Shakespeare a different story from the memory that made you shiver?"

"Nope. It's the same one."

Granuaile clapped her hands together and made a tiny squeaking noise, which made Oberon thump his tail on the ground.

What are you getting excited about? I asked him.

<I don't know, Atticus, but she sounds really happy so I'm happy for her. Did people in England have poodles back then?>

They might have, but I didn't see any.

<Oh, I'm sorry, Atticus. That must have been rough on you. I know it's been rough on me, out here all alone without any asses to sniff—>

I know, buddy, I know, we need to go into town soon so you can have a social life.

<I will dream of it! But after we eat. Which I hope is now.>

Looking across the fire at Granuaile, I said, "Oberon's happy for you. He'd be even happier if we ate before I get into the story."

"Sounds good to me. It should be ready, don't you think?"

I nodded, fetched three bowls, and ladled out the lamb stew for each of us, cautioning Oberon to let it cool a little first so he wouldn't burn his tongue.

"So were you in England the whole time Shakespeare was writing?"

"No, I missed the reign of Queen Elizabeth entirely and arrived from Japan shortly after her death."

"What were you doing in Japan?"

"That's a story for another night, but it was an exciting time. I saw the establishment of the Tokugawa shogunate and witnessed early stages of the construction of Nijo Castle in Kyoto. But Aenghus Óg eventually found me there and I had to move, and I chose to move much closer to home because an English sailor had told me of this Shakespeare character. My interest was piqued."

<Wasn't England composed primarily of fleas at that time?>

"Yes, Oberon. It was mostly fleas and excrement in the streets and people dying of consumption and Catholics and Protestants hating each other. Quite different from Japan. But Shakespeare made it all bearable somehow."

"Kind of makes his work even more amazing when you think about it," Granuaile commented. "You don't read *Hamlet* and think, 'This man could not avoid stepping in shit every day of his life.'"

"It was also difficult at that time to move around London without passing within hexing distance of a witch."

"They were truly that common back then?"

"Aye. And their existence wasn't even a question; people in those days knew witchcraft to be a fact as surely as they knew their teeth ached. And King James fancied himself quite the witch hunter, you know. Wrote a book about it."

"I didn't realize that."

"Of course, the kind of witches you might run into—and warlocks too, we shouldn't pretend that only women engaged in such practices—varied widely. For many it was a taste of power that the medieval patriarchy wouldn't otherwise allow them."

"Can't say that I blame them. If you don't give people a conventional path to power they will seek out their own unconventional path."

"Said the Druid's apprentice," I teased.

"That's right. I'm sticking it to the Man!" Granauile said, extending a middle finger to the sky.

<Yeah!> Oberon said, and barked once for Granuaile's benefit, adding in a tail wag.

"Well, the witches that almost ended Shakespeare certainly wanted to stick it to him."

"Is this why there's a curse on *Macbeth*? You're not supposed to say its name or bad luck will befall you, right, so actors always call it 'the Scottish play' or something?"

"Almost, yes. The way the legend goes, the witches were upset that Shakespeare wrote down their real spells and they wanted the play suppressed because of it—hence the curse."

"Those weren't real spells?" Granuaile asked, lifting a spoonful of stew to her mouth.

"No, but Shakespeare thought they were. What angered the witches was his portrayal of Hecate."

My apprentice stopped mid-slurp and actually choked a little bit, losing a little bit of stew. "You and Shakespeare met Hecate?"

"That's a polite way of putting it, but yes. I met her and the three witches, and so did Shakespeare, and that inspired portions of what many now call the Scottish play."

My apprentice grinned and let loose with another squee of excitement. "Okay, okay, I can't wait, but I want to finish this stew first. Because I slurp and Oberon turbo-slurps."

Oberon's laps at the bowl really were loud enough to blot out all other nearby sound.

<She's right. I take a back seat to no one at slurping,> Oberon said.

When we'd all finished, Oberon curled up at my feet where I could pet him easily, Granuaile and I thumbed open some cold ones, and the crackle of the logs under the stewpot provided occasional exclamation points to my tale.

In 1604 I arrived in London, paid two pennies and witnessed a performance of *Othello* in the Globe Theatre. It smelled foul—they had no toilets in the facility, you know, so people just dropped a deuce wherever they could find space—but the play was divine. That's when I knew the rumored genius of Shakespeare was an absolute fact. Poetry and pathos and an astounding villain in the form of Iago—I was more than merely impressed. I knew that he was a bard worthy of the ancient Druidic bards of my youth, and I simply had to meet him.

The way to meet almost anyone you wanted in London was to wear expensive clothing and pretend to be French. Clothing equaled money and money opened all doors, and pretending to be French kept them from checking up on me easily while allowing me to misunderstand questions I didn't want to answer. I dyed my hair black, shaved my beard into something foppish and pointy, and inquired at the Merchant Taylors Hall on Threadneedle Street where I might find a tailor to dress me properly. They gave me a name and address, and I arrived there with a purse full of coin and a French accent, calling myself Jacques Lefebvre, the Marquis de Crèvecoeur in Picardy. That was all it took to establish one's identity in those days. If you had the means to appear wealthy and noble then everyone accepted that you were. And the bonuses to being one of the nobility were that I could openly wear Fragarach and get away with wearing gloves all the time. The triskele tattoo on the back of my right hand would raise far too many questions otherwise. To the Jacobeans there was functionally no difference between a Druid and a witch: If it was magic, their solution was to kill it with fire.

It is now well known that Shakespeare rented rooms from a French couple in Cripplegate in 1604, but it took me some time back then to find that out. Though I heard from several sources that he was "around Cripplegate," no one would tell me precisely where he lived. That was no matter: All I had to do was ask about him in several Cripplegate establishments and eventually he found me. Helpful neighbors, no doubt, who could not for ready money remember where he lived, shot off to inform him straightaway after speaking with me that a Frenchman with a fat purse was asking about him. He found me nursing a cup of wine in a tavern. I was careful to order the quality stuff instead of sack or small beer. Appearances were quite important at the time, and Shakespeare was well aware. He had taken the trouble to groom himself and wash his clothing before bowing at my table and begging my pardon, but might I be the Marquis de Crévecoeur?

He wore a black tunic sewn with vertical lines of silver thread and punctuated with occasional pinpoints of embroidery. His collar was large but not one of those ridiculous poufy ruffs you saw in those later portraits of him. Those portraits—engravings, really—were done after his death in preparation for the publishing of his plays. In the flesh he looked very similar to the Sanders portrait they found in Canada, painted just the year before I met him. His beard and mustache were soft, wispy things trimmed short, a sop to fashion but clearly not something he cared about. His hair, brown and fine, formed a slightly frazzled cloud around his skull, and he almost always had a smirk playing about his lips. He was neither handsome nor ugly, but the intelligence that shone behind those brown eyes was impossible to miss.

"Oui?" I said, affecting a French accent. It was more south-of-France rather than genuine Picardy, but I was hoping Englishmen would be unable to tell the difference the same way that most modern Americans cannot distinguish the regional differences between English accents.

"I'm told you've been looking for me," he said. "I'm Master William Shakespeare of the King's Men."

"Ah! Excellent, Monsieur, I have indeed been asking about you! I wish to pay my respects; I just saw *Othello* recently and was astounded by your skill. How like you this establishment?" I said, for it was fair-to-middling shabby and I had chosen it for its visibility more than its reputation. "May I buy you a bottle of wine here or do you prefer a more, ah, how do you say, exquisite cellar?"

"I know of an excellent establishment if you would not mind a walk," he replied, and so it was that I settled my bill, allowing my coin-heavy purse to be viewed, and navigated the standing shit of Jacobean London to the White Hart Inn, the courtyard of which had played host to Shakespeare's company under Queen Elizabeth, when his troupe was called the Lord Chamberlain's Men.

Though it was April, the skies permitted little in the way of warmth and that gave me some excuse to keep my gloves on. I played the fawning patron of the arts and so I enjoyed my evening at the White Hart Inn where Master Shakespeare was well known. He ordered a bottle of good wine and put it on my tab, and it wasn't long before he was talking about his current projects. Since King James himself was his patron he could hardly set aside projects meant for him and do something specifically for me, but he could certainly discuss his work and perhaps, for a generous donation to the King's Men, work in something that would please my eyes and ears.

"I'm quite near to finishing *King Lear*," he said, "and I have in mind something that might appeal at court, a Scottish skullduggery from a century or so past. A thane called Macbeth aspires to murder his way to the throne. But this exposure of a thane's base ambition is lacking something."

"What? A knavery? A scandalous liaison?"

"Something of the supernatural," he said, lowering his voice as one does when discussing the vaguely spooky. "The King possesses a keen interest for such things and it behooves me to please the royal audience. But I confess myself unacquainted with sufficient occult knowledge to inform my writing. There's my astrologer, of course, but he knows little of darker matters and he's a gossip besides."

"Do you need first-hand knowledge to write about it? Can you not glean what inspiration you need from others?"

Shakespeare shook his head, finished his cup of wine and poured a refill from the bottle on the table. "Ah, M'sieur Lefebvre, what I've read is too fantastical to be believed, and I do not wish to tread on ground so well-packed by others. I need something compelling, a spectacle to grab you firmly in the nethers and refuse to let go. Even the fabulous must have been kissed by reality at some point to have the blush of truth, and without that blush it will not work in theatre."

"Have you any idea where to find such spectacle?"

The Bard leaned forward conspiratorially. "I do have an inkling. It is a new moon tonight, and I have heard tales that on such nights, north of town in Finsbury Fields, black arts are practiced."

I snorted. "Black arts? Who would report such things? If one were truly involved one would hardly spread word of it and invite a burning at the stake. And if one witnessed such rites up close it follows that one would hardly survive it."

"No, no, you misunderstand: These accounts speak of strange unholy fires spied in the darkness and the distant cackling of hags."

"Bah. Improbable fiction," I declared, waving it away as folly.

"Most like. But suppose, M'sieur Lefebvre, that it is not? What meat for my art might I find out there?" The innkeeper delivered a board of cheese, bread and sausage to the table and

Shakespeare speared a grey link that had been boiled a bit too enthusiastically. He held it up between us and eyed it with dismay. "One would hope it would be better fare than this."

"Will you go a-hunting, then?"

Shakespeare pounded the table once with the flat of his left palm and pointed at me, amused at a sudden thought. "We shall go together."

I nearly choked and coughed to clear my throat before spluttering, "What? Are you addle-pated?"

"You have a sword. I'll bring a torch. If we find nothing it will still be a pleasant walk in the country."

"But if we find something we could well lose our souls."

"My most excellent Marquis, I have every confidence that you will protect me long enough to make good my escape." His grin was so huge that I could not help but laugh.

"I trust you would give me a hero's death in your next play."

"Aye, you would be immortalized in verse!"

I kept him waiting while I decided: If we actually found a genuine coven cooking up something out there in the fields, it could prove to be a terrible evening—they tended to put everything from asshole cats to cat assholes in their stews, simply horrifying ingredients to construct their bindings and exert their will upon nature since they weren't already bound to it like I was. But the risk, while real, was rather small.

"Very well, I'll go. But I think it might be wiser to go a-horseback, so that we both might have a chance of outrunning anything foul. Can you ride?"

"I can."

And so it was settled. We ate overboiled meat and drank more wine and I allowed myself to enjoy the buzz for a while, but when it was time for us to depart I triggered my healing charm to break down the poison of alcohol in my blood. Some people might be comfortable witch hunting under the influence but I was not. I arranged with a stable to borrow some horses and late at night, under the dark of a new moon, went looking for the worst kind of trouble with William Shakespeare.

By the time we set out his cheeks were flushed and he was a far cry from sober, but neither was he so impaired that he could not stay in the saddle—writers and their livers.

The smoke and fog and sewer stench of London followed us out of the city proper to Finsbury Fields, which are simply suburbs, a park, and St. Luke's church now, but which were liberally fertilized with all manner of excrescence back then and some had been gamely sown with attempted crops. Muddy wagon trails divided the fields and it was Shakespeare's idea that we would find the hags at some crossroads out there, if the rumors of witchcraft were true.

"On the continent one can still find offerings left at crossroads on the new moon for Hecate, or Trivium," he said, and I feigned ignorance of the custom.

"Is that so? I have never heard the like."

"Oh, aye. It is always at three roads, however, not four; Hecate has a triple aspect."

"So we are looking for worshippers of Hecate, then?"

"The proceedings being held on the new moon would be consistent with her cult. It is a slightly different devilry from dealing with powers of hell, but no less damned."

I suppressed a smile at that. The worship of Hecate had taken many forms throughout the centuries—her conception and manifestation was especially fluid compared to that of most other deities. Even today she is the patron goddess of some Wiccans, who look at her as embodying the maiden-mother-crone tradition, a gentler conception than the sometimes fierce and bloodthirsty manifestations she took on in earlier days.

Shakespeare, of course, looked upon all witches, regardless of type, through the Christian filter—evil by default and allied with hell to destroy Christendom. I looked at them through the Druidic filter: plenty of witches were fine in my book until they tried to twist nature's powers for their own purposes. If they wanted to curse someone with bad luck or sacrifice a goat with a knife to summon a demon, that was their business and frankly not my fight. I was also grateful for those who tried to heal others or craft wards against malevolent spirits. But moon magic could be dangerous, and attempts to bind weather or possess people or animals would draw my annoyed attention rather quickly. The elementals would let me know what was up and I would come running.

It was because of this that I tended not to notice the benevolent witches or even meet them very often; they did their thing in secret and harmed no one. All I ever saw were the bad apples and it probably prejudiced me against witches in general over time.

The dirt tracks cutting swaths through Finsbury Fields were not precisely dry but neither were they muddy bogs. They'd be dry in another day or so and the horses left only soft depressions in the mud, chopping up the ruts somewhat and moving quietly at a slow walk. The rustle of our clothes and our conversation made more noise than the horses' hooves.

That noise, however, was enough to attract four figures out of the darkness—that and Shakespeare's torch, no doubt.

"Please, good sir, could you give me directions?" a voice said in the night. We reined in—a terrible decision—and four unshaven and aggressively unwashed men with atrocious dentition approached from either side of our horses, taking reins with one hand and pointing daggers at us with the other. A very smooth and practiced waylay, and they knew it. We could not move without being cut, and they smiled up at us with blackened, ravaged teeth, enjoying our expressions of surprise and dismay.

The leader was on my right and spoke again. "More specifically, can you direct me to your purse? Hand it over now and we'll let you be on your way, there's a good lad."

If it had been only coins in my purse I would have happily obliged. Coins are easy to come by. But the piece of cold iron resting in the bottom was rare and I didn't wish to part with it.

Shakespeare, who was not only deep in his cups but thrashing about deeply in them, began hurling insults at the leader, who found them rather amusing and smiled indulgently at the angry sot while never taking his eyes off me.

"You raw and chap-blistered rhinoceros tit!" Shakespeare roared. "You onion-fed pustule of a snarling badger quim! How dare you accost the Marquis de Crèvecoeur!"

The bandit laughed, polluting the air with his halitosis. I began to mutter bindings in Old Irish to increase my strength and speed, drawing on the stored energy in my bear charm, which they would probably interpret as nervous French. "Visiting from the continent, are we? Well, me chapped tits and snarling quim would welcome some French coin as well as English."

His companions chuckled at his lame riposte, confident that they had the better of us, and the one on my left with a broken nose and a boil on his cheek gestured with his dagger. "Let's begin with you getting off that high horse, Marquis."

Shakespeare wouldn't let that pass without loud comment, still directing his remarks at the man on my right. "Cease and begone, villain! You have all the dignity of a flea-poxed cur's crusty pizzle! You dry, pinched anus of a Puritan preacher!"

Their gap-toothed smiles instantly transformed into scowls and all eyes swung to the bard. "What!" The leader barked. "Did he just call me a bloody Puritan?"

"Not exactly," Cheek Boil said. "I think he called you a Puritan's bunghole."

While keeping his hand on my horse's bridle, the leader swung his dagger away from my thigh to point at Will behind me. "Listen, you shite, I may be a bunghole," he cried, brown phlegmy spittle flying from his maw, "but I'm a proper God-fearing one, not some frothy Puritan baggage!"

While they were all looking at Will, I triggered my camouflage charm, taking on the pigments of my surrounding and effectively disappearing in the dim torchlight. Using the boosted strength and speed I'd drawn, I slipped my left foot out of the stirrup and kicked Cheek Boil in the chest before falling to the right and landing chops on either end of the leader's collarbones. They broke, he dropped both his knife and my horse's reins, and

I gave him a head butt in the face to make sure he fell backward and stayed there.

My attack drew the attention of the men watching the Bard, and he was not slow to seize advantage of the opportunity. With the gazes of the two men pulled forward, he dipped the torch in his left hand and shoved it into the face of the man on his left. He screamed and dropped his weapon, stepping back with both hands clutched to his eyes. That startled Shakespeare's horse and it shied and whinnied, ripping out of the grip of the rogue on Shakespeare's right. He began shouting, "Oi! Hey!" and then, seeing that his companions were all wounded or down and he wasn't either quite yet, he muttered, "To hell with this," and scarpered off whence he came, into the dark wet sludge of Finsbury Fields. The leader was discovering how difficult it was to get up with a couple of broken collarbones and called for help. Cheek Boil, who'd not been seriously hurt, recovered and moved to help him, not seeing me.

Fire Face, meanwhile, had morphed from mean to murderous. Nothing would do for him now but to bury his knife in Shakespeare's guts. Growling as he searched for the knife he dropped in the dark, I scrambled in front of Will's horse, dropping my camouflage as I did so, and drew Fragarach, slipping in between Will and Fire Face just as he found his knife and reared up in triumph.

"Think carefully, Englishman," I said, doing my best to emphasize that I was very French and not an Irish lad.

Fire Face was not a spectacular thinker. He was a ginger like me, perhaps prone to impetuousness, and he bellowed to intimidate me and charged. Maybe his plan was to wait for me to swing or stab and then try to duck or dodge, get in close, and shove that dagger into my guts. Perhaps it would have worked against someone with normal reflexes. I slashed him across the chest, drawing a red line across his torso, and he dropped to the ground and screamed all out of proportion to the wound, "O! O! I am slain!"

"Oh, shut up," I spat. "You are not. You're just stupid, that's all." Turning to Will, I said, "Ride ahead a short distance, Master Shakespeare. I will be close behind." I slapped the rump of his horse and it surged forward despite the protests of its rider. I kept Fragarach out and stepped around my horse to check on Cheek Boil and the leader. Cheek Boil was trying to help the leader to his feet but was having trouble without an arm to pull on. The pigeon-livered one who ran away could neither be seen nor heard.

"I'm leaving you alive, monsieurs," I said as I sheathed my sword and mounted my horse. "A favor that you would not likely have extended to me. Think kinder of the French from now on, yes?"

A torrent of fairly creative profanity and the continued wailing of Fire Face trailed me as I goaded the horse to catch up to Will, but I was glad I didn't have to kill any of them. William Shakcspcarc would probably cxaggcratc thc cncountcr as it was and I didn't need a reputation as a duelist or fighter of any kind.

The Bard was jubilant when I caught up to him. "Excellent fighting, Marquis! You moved so quickly I lost track of you for a moment!"

Ignoring that reference to my brief time in camouflage, I said, "You were quite skilled with the torch."

Shakespeare grinned at it, jiggling it a little in his fist. "And it's still aflame! Finest torch I've ever carried."

"Shall we return to London, then?"

"What, already? Fie! That passing distraction is no matter. We have hags to find."

"I doubt we will find them in these fields. It seems to be populated by villains and pale vegetables, and fortune may not favor us a second time."

"Tush! Think no more on it! You are more than a match for any bandits, M'sieur Lefebvre."

"I may not be a match for one with a bow."

"Anyone skilled with a bow would be patrolling a richer stretch of road than a wagon trail in this mildewed fen, M'sieur."

He had a point, damn him. Using one of my charms—newly completed at that time—I cast night vision as a precaution and didn't look toward the torch anymore. If another set of bandits wished to ambush us I would see them coming. I was so intent at scanning the area on the right side of the road that Shakespeare startled me after a half mile by saying, "There." He pointed off to his left and I had to lean forward and crane my neck to see what he was looking at. It was a faint white glow on the horizon, a nimbus of weak light in the darkness near the ground. It flickered as if something passed in front of it and kept moving. "What could that be?" he asked. "'Tis the wrong color of light for a campfire, wouldn't you say?"

I grunted noncommittally but could think of no good reason to ignore it. I followed Shakespeare's horse once we came to a track that appeared to lead directly to the light.

As we drew closer we could hear chanting floating over the fen, and I realized that we might have actually found the witches Shakespeare was hoping to find and I was hoping not to. There would be no telling him to turn back while I investigated on my own—and I *did* need to investigate in case their ritual proved to be an attempt to usurp some measure of the earth's magic. But I couldn't risk revealing myself as a Druid to him if I was forced to act. I would be every bit as damned in his eyes as the witches if he discovered my pagan origins.

We dismounted to creep forward on foot. I doubted the horses would still be there when we returned but we couldn't take them with us; even though they were quieter than usual in the soft earth, they weren't stealthy creatures. One impatient snort could give us away.

Keeping my voice low, I said, "Conceal the torch behind my body," and watching him step uncertainly in the mud, still quite drunk, I added, "preferably without setting me aflame. It will allow us to see while hopefully preventing our detection."

"I approve of this plan," he said, enunciating carefully, and we stepped forward into the mud, the macabre sounds of muted chanting pounding nails of dread into our hearts. With every step nearer I grew more certain that we had, in fact, discovered a small coven of witches. The light was indeed from some kind of fire but the wood wasn't burning orange and yellow as it should. It was silvery like moonlight. Perhaps there was phosphorus at work. Or something arcane.

I began to worry about Shakespeare's safety. I had my cold iron amulet tucked underneath my tunic to protect me against magic, but the Bard had nothing. I wanted to tell him I had protection but couldn't tell him I had bound the cold iron to my aura. I had to craft a lie that he would accept. "Master Shakespeare, should we be discovered, let me go ahead. I have a blessed talisman that may shield me against their, ah, infernal practices." I wasn't sure where he stood on the Holy Roman Church so I settled for the generic "blessed" rather than "Pope-licked" or "Cardinal-kissed" or any number of other vaguely holy-sounding phrases. I drew Fragarach from its scabbard. "I also have this, should it be necessary."

Shakespeare's breathing was coming quicker and his eyes had widened. "Your plans continue to be well-conceived, Marquis."

We continued to creep closer, the voices growing louder and a faint rumble and hiss could be heard, which I imagined to be something boiling in the cauldron. It was a large black iron affair, the sort one uses to feed armies and usually transported in a wagon, and I could only imagine how they had lugged it out there and what might be boiling inside of it. Perhaps the darkness concealed an ox and cart nearby. The unnatural white flames glowed underneath it and licked at the sides, consuming what appeared to be normal firewood.

As we drew close enough to distinguish words I recognized that the chanting was in Greek, which Shakespeare did not understand but I understood very well. I chose to be a classically educated Marquis and translated for the Bard in whispers when he asked me if I could make sense of their babble.

"It's an invocation to Hecate, pleading for her guidance—no. Her *personal* guidance. As in guiding them, in person, right here! They are trying to summon her."

"A summoning! For what purpose?"

"I know not."

We were close enough now that I, with my aided vision, could distinguish shapes in the darkness—I doubted that Shakespeare could see anything except that something kept moving in front of the firelight.

There were three witches circling the cauldron, naked but smeared with streaks of something dark—blood or animal fat would be my guess. Their ages were indeterminate; by appearance they were somewhere on the happy side of middle age but I knew that in reality they could be much older than that. As they circled the fire they also spun around themselves, raising their arms and voices to the sky. I wondered how they kept from getting dizzy.

Their right hands each held a short dagger—no special curved blades or gilded guards, nothing you might call an athame—they were merely sharp, efficient knives.

"Master Shakespeare," I whispered, "they are armed and I do not doubt they will attack if provoked. We should probably keep our distance."

"How can you see anything, Marquis? I can only see shadows in the dark. My eyes need some assistance and I must see better; this could prove to be a fine provocative sauce for my play."

I could hardly cast night vision on him without revealing my abilities, so I sighed and said, "If we're going to get any closer I suggest you put out that torch."

I expected a protest but he complied instantly, jamming it into the mud behind me. He dearly wanted to get a closer look; to this point he hadn't seen nearly so much as I had.

We inched forward, ignoring the filthy ground, fascinated by the lights and the ritual playing out before us. I was fairly certain by then that I would have no official role to play as a protector of the earth, but playing protector to Shakespeare could be even more dangerous if we were discovered.

The cauldron, I noticed, squatted in the middle of a crossroads, but the three-way sort to which Shakespeare alluded earlier. What possible need the witches could have for Hecate's personal appearance I could not imagine. Their hair was tied and queued behind them and I perceived that they wore theatre masks straight out of ancient Greece, albeit the visages of bearded men strangely attached to what were plainly female bodies. Masked rites might make them Thracians, but if so their presence in England was especially bewildering.

The only possible motivation I could come up with to conduct such a ritual near London was the upset or even overthrow of King James's reign, but I was surprised that Greek cultists would care about it. Perhaps they didn't care but were doing this on a mercenary basis—I had heard there were plots boiling all over the country, but mostly by Catholics opposed to King James' very existence. We were only twenty months away from the Guy Fawkes Gunpowder Plot, after all. But if those witches were Catholic then I was the son of a goat.

"What token of hell is this?" Shakespeare breathed next to me, his eyes wide and fixed on the spectacle. We were crouched low to the ground on our haunches. "Bearded women cavorting and, and…" He fell speechless. Sometimes there simply aren't words, even for him.

"Draw no closer," I warned him, listening to their chant. "Their words have changed. The invocation is set and now they are waiting."

"What are they saying?"

"They are literally saying that they are waiting. *Periménoume* means 'we wait' and they're just repeating that, spinning around."

"For what do they wait?"

"My guess would be a sacrifice. Maybe they know we're here and they're waiting for us to get closer, and then they will sacrifice us to their goddess."

Shakespeare did not fall for my scare tactics. "Did they not sacrifice something already? There has to be something in that cauldron."

"Aye, but a chicken or a newt will not summon a goddess to English shores. It will only secure a flicker of her attention. They need something bigger."

"How know you this?"

"I am a witch hunter of sorts myself," I said, "though I confess I did not expect to find any tonight."

"You doubted me, M'sieur?"

"No, I doubted the stories you heard." But now that I heard the witches were "waiting," I wondered how long they had been coming out here during the new moon to wait. Those stories of lights and croaking hags looked to be true now.

"Why not simply bring the necessary sacrifices with them?" Shakespeare asked.

"It is a matter of power," I said. "If the sacrifices come to the crossroads willingly it would be better for their purposes."

Behind us, we heard the neigh of a horse—quite probably one of ours. The witches heard it too. They didn't stop their chanting or their ritualistic circling of the cauldron, but their masked faces pointed in that direction—in our direction, in fact. I didn't have to tell Shakespeare that he shouldn't say another word. We emulated the movement and speech of stone gargoyles in the darkness and kept our eyes on the coven.

Soon the approach of hooves reached our ears, a soft rumbling thump in the mud, and an angry voice shouted, "That has to be them up ahead, or someone who saw where they went!"

It sounded like Fire Face to me. Apparently he had recovered from thinking I had slain him and now he wanted a piece of both of us. Chucking Will on the shoulder, I gestured that we should get off the road, and we rolled in the mud until we were naturally (rather than magically) camouflaged in a sodden field of disconsolate cabbages.

It was Fire Face, all right, riding my horse, and riding double on Will's were Cheek Boil and Pigeon Liver, a surprise guest. The latter must have returned and offered to make up for his earlier cowardice. And Fire Face's spleen must have been full of rage to pursue us so blindly and abandon their leader somewhere behind. Fire Face was the *de facto* leader now, and clearly not expecting to find three naked, masked, and dancing witches at a crossroads in Finsbury Fields. The leader had been left behind with his broken collarbones and were he there to witness what happened next, he would have counted himself fortunate.

The witches stopped chanting "We wait" and each said in turn, "The time is now," and then, in concert, "Hecate comes!"

The bandits reined in short of the fire, and Cheek Boil exclaimed, "What the bloody hell?" shortly before it all became a bloody hell.

I sat up to yank off my right boot so that the binding tattoo on the sole of my foot could contact the earth and allow me to draw upon its energy. The witches broke their circle and streaked directly at the horses, knives held high and moving much faster than humans should. I would need to speed up just to match them.

"What are these naked wenches?" Fire Face said, and then one leapt straight over his horse's head to tackle him backwards out of the saddle. Cheek Boil and Pigeon Liver were similarly bowled over and the horses bolted, not bred or trained for war. The strength of the witches became evident in the next few seconds as they stood each bandit up and employed those knives, drawing them across the men's throats with an audible slice of flesh. As their life's blood gouted into the mud and they tried in vain to staunch the flow with their hands, the witches dragged them to the crossroads in front of the cauldron, then pushed them into a triangle formed by their shoulder blades, each one of them facing a different direction.

"Come to us, Hecate, Queen of the Moon!" they cried. "Your vessels await!"

"Oh, no," I said, and rose to my feet, drawing Fragarach. They really were going to summon her.

Shakespeare would have joined me, no doubt, but was trying to vomit quietly on the cabbage instead. His earlier drinking had soured his stomach and seeing a murder so starkly committed brought a good measure of it back up.

I couldn't reach the witches in time to stop the summoning and I had Shakespeare to worry about, so I had to watch. We'd be leaving as soon as he finished emptying his guts. The bandits began to twitch, then shudder, then buck violently against the staying hands of the witches on their sternums; their eyes rolled up in their heads and their tongues lolled out of their mouths while blood continued to squirt from their carotids. And then it all stopped for a second, the air charged and the hairs on the back of my neck started like the quills of the fretful porpentine, for Hecate slipped out of whatever netherworld plane she'd been occupying and into the bodies of those three bandits, simultaneously her sacrifices and her new vessels. Their lives were forfeit, their spirits expelled who knows where, and Triple Hecate had new flesh to command far from Thrace.

Except she didn't much like the look or feel of that flesh—it was male, for one thing. So she set about changing it to suit her, and that was when Shakespeare looked up from his retching to see what else could horrify him.

The witches stepped back from the bodies since it was Hecate occupying them now and they stood on their own power. But the skin of the men's faces split and melted as it changed shape, and muted popping noises indicated that their very bones were being broken and reformed to suit the will of the goddess. The Bard did me an enormous favor at that point and fainted into the cabbage patch after a single squeak of abject terror. It meant I wouldn't have to pretend to be a French nobleman anymore or hide my abilities.

His squeak, however, did catch the attention of one of the witches, and she was just able to spy me and hiss a challenge into the night. "Who is there?" she said in accented English.

The other two swiveled their heads at that, and the one who had killed Cheek Boil said in Greek, "I will look. Hecate must not be disturbed in transition."

She darted in my direction, bloody knife out, as I was thinking that perhaps Hecate *should* be disturbed in transition. Any aspect of the goddess summoned in this manner would fail spectacularly on measurements of benevolence and goodwill. Deities that manifest through animal and human sacrifice tend not to engage in acts of philanthropy.

The witch located me and rushed forward, no doubt assuming that I was as slow as the bandits had been. But I was not only as fast as she but better armed and better trained. Her unguarded lunge, meant to dispatch me quickly, got her arm lopped off at the wrist and a face-first trip into the mud. Her mask crunched and she howled, cradling her shortened arm with her good one. She was far too close to Shakespeare for my comfort, though she hadn't seen him yet. The wisest thing for my own safety would be to cast camouflage and disappear, but they might find and slay William while searching for me, so I kept myself visible and moved purposely away from him to the other side of the road, which looked like a turnip field. The witches all tracked me, and the one I'd wounded pointed with her good hand.

"He's not human!" she shouted in Greek. "He moves like us!"

"I'm a Druid of Gaia," I announced in the same language. If Shakespeare revived and heard any of this my cover wouldn't be blown. "I mean you no harm if you mean no harm to the earth."

"No harm!" the wounded witch shrieked. "You cut off my hand!"

"You were trying to kill me with it," I pointed out. "And I chose to maim when I could have killed. Considering what you've just done to those men I think I have the moral high ground." The hot waxen features of the former bandits was slowing, congealing, solidifying into female faces, and their hair was growing long and dark at an alarming rate; their frames shrunk somewhat in their clothing as they transformed into feminine figures. "Isn't talking more pleasant? Let's chat. Why are you summoning Hecate here?"

"The Druids died out long ago," one near the fire said, ignoring my question.

"It's funny you say that because I was going to say there were no Thracian witches in England."

With a final crescendo of chunky bone noises and a slurp of sucking flesh, Hecate finished transforming the bodies of her vessels into her preferred manifestation and three women who could have stepped off a Grecian urn—long noses, thin lips, flawless skin, and all kinds of kohl on the eyelids—took deep breaths and exhaled as one. They weren't of differing ages in the mold of maiden-mother-crone: They could be teenaged triplets, which made sense since it was really a single goddess in there and I regret now that I never asked her if she took pleasure in confounding storytellers with the problem of whether to use singular or plural pronouns. I'll stick with plural for the moment because after the synchronized sigh that the witches and I all simply watched in awe, their eyes fluttered open and they spoke in creepy unison, "Blood."

That was a pretty dire omen, but it got worse. Triple Hecate's heads swung to look directly at me and smiled. "His will do. Bring me his heart."

Her hands shot in my direction and she spat, *"Pétra ostá!"* which meant *stone bones*. She wanted me to stand petrified while her witches carved me up, but her hex ran into my cold iron aura and fizzled, resulting in nothing more than a thump of my amulet against my chest. I played along with it, though, freezing up, widening my eyes and warbling in panic as the two healthy witches raced forward to do Hecate's bidding. Had they been the least bit cautious—a lesson they should have learned after the experience their sister had in coming after me—I might not have been able to handle two at once. But they came in unguarded, unable to fathom the idea that their goddess's powers might have a counter or a limit.

Still, I didn't kill them. They were too undisciplined to be a true threat, but since I couldn't have them ganging up on me either, they each got a slash across the belly to make them sit down and work on healing for a while. If they were half decent at witchcraft—their accomplishments suggested they were—they'd eventually be fine, but it would take them a while. And then the easy part was over.

Triple Hecate, unlike her witches, was very disciplined and knew how to coordinate the attacks of her vessels. And she was able to juice up those bodies even more than I was, though I didn't know at first what fuel she was using for it; if it was blood then she would need more soon, and Shakespeare was still available. Hissing, she launched herself at me and spread herself out, two of her vessels flanking me and dodging my first swing. Lunging forward in coordinated strikes and dancing out of the way of my blade, I got a kick in the kidney, a hammer blow to the ribs that cracked one, and a breath-stealing punt to the diaphragm before I remembered to trigger my camouflage. She had a more difficult time targeting me after that and couldn't track the sword but still got her licks in because I fell down and she heard it, aiming her kicks low. I was able to get in a few of mine, though. Fragarach was able to cut her a few times, never deeply, but she slowed noticeably after each one. She really did need that blood to fuel her speed and strength; she wasn't feeding on the life energy of the earth but rather the energy of sacrifices.

The dismembered witch, whom I'd forgotten about, cried out in discovery. "Queen Hecate! There's a man asleep over here! His blood will set you right!"

Triple Hecate backed off and turned away, and I looked as well to see the witch pointing with her good hand toward Shakespeare. There was no way I'd be able to get up and run over there faster than Hecate.

I swung quick and hard with everything I had at the legs of the nearest vessel, taking off a foot and chunking into the other leg, but the other two dashed off to feed on the Bard. While my target fell over and I rose to my knees, gasping for breath, the other two called for a knife to cut Shakespeare's throat.

"I lost mine in the mud," the witch wailed, her voice making it plain that she feared Hecate's displeasure.

"Check your belts," one of the other witches moaned, reminding Hecate that her vessels had been wearing clothes and yes, weapons. As one—including mine—the vessels looked down, spied their daggers, and drew them. The mobile vessels were closing on Shakespeare and would end him in seconds. There was no time for subtlety, only a desperate chance at saving him. Scrambling on my hand and knees to the fallen vessel, which she heard, I thrust upward into her skull from the bottom of her jaw just underneath the chin, shoving through into the brain and scrambling any chance of healing that particular mortal coil. At the same time, she stabbed into my vulnerable left side with her newfound dagger, sinking it below my armpit into a lung. I collapsed on top of her as she expired and I heard a cry in stereo: The other two vessels stopped, shook as if gripped by a seizure, and then exploded in a shower of chunky meat and bone.

It had worked—though on a significantly more gory level than I expected: Triple Hecate could not occupy only two vessels. Kill one and you kill them all.

Or you hit the reset button, anyway. I was under no illusion that Hecate had really been slain; she'd merely been banished to whatever Olympian ether she'd come from, and she could be summoned again, though I imagined it would be difficult.

A hush born of shock settled about the field for a few seconds, and then the weird sisters shrieked—and not over their various wounds. They'd toiled and waited a long time for their moment, for whatever reason, and most likely thought Hecate invincible. To see all of that crushed in the space of minutes caused them more than a little emotional distress.

Wincing, I yanked out the knife in my side and triggered my healing charm, drawing plenty of power through the earth to fuel it. It would take a while to heal but I felt sure I'd survive; I still had doubts about Shakespeare. The first witch was standing over him and might kill him out of spite. Lurching to my feet was impossible to do quietly and the witches all turned at the sound. They couldn't make me out but knew I was there.

"We will curse you for this, Druid," one of them promised. She was clutching her guts together in the mud.

"You can try, but it would be a waste of your time," I said. "If Hecate's curse didn't work on me, why would yours?"

They didn't have a ready answer for that, so they took turns suggesting various sex acts I could perform with animals and I let them. The longer their attention was focused on me and my words the closer I staggered to Shakespeare. I goaded them a couple times to keep them going, and then, when I was close enough, I poked the first witch with the tip of Fragarach, just a nick, and that caused her to yelp and leap away from him. She cradled her stump, which I noticed she had managed to stop bleeding. I stepped forward, placing myself between her and the Bard's prone form, and dropped my camouflage.

"Hi. Back away, join your sisters, and you can live. You might even summon Hecate again someday. Or I can kill you now. What'll it be?"

She said nothing but retreated, always keeping her eyes on me, and I watched her go, keeping my guard up.

With a little bit of help from the elemental communicating through the earth, I located the horses—they hadn't run far—and convinced them that they'd be safe if they returned to give us a ride back to town; when we got to the stables they'd get oats and apples.

While I waited for them, I knelt and checked on Shakespeare. He was unharmed except for his drunken oblivion; he'd likely have a monstrous hangover. But while he was out of immediate physical danger, he still needed magical protection. The witches might not be able to curse me but they could curse him and it would occur to them to try before I left the field. But the piece of cold iron in my purse that I'd been anxious to hold onto earlier would do me yeoman service now. I fished it out, and having no string or chain on me, bound it to his skin at the hollow of his throat and made it a talisman against direct hexes. It wouldn't save him from more carefully crafted curses using his blood or hair, but I'd address that next.

The witches huddled together and eyed me through their bearded masks as I hefted Shakespeare over his horse's back, a task made more difficult with my wound. I did what I could to hide his face from their view and was particularly careful about leaving anything behind for them to use against us later. I located Shakespeare's vomit and my blood, and with the elemental's aid made sure that everything got turned into the earth and buried deep.

I snuffed out the fire too, binding dirt to the wood to smother the unnatural flames, and that not only left the crossroads really dark but it prevented the witches from doing much else that night, and they complained loudly that they needed it to heal.

"Don't try to summon Hecate in England again," I called over their cursing, giving the horses a mental nudge to walk on. "England and Ireland are under my protection. I won't be so merciful a second time."

A tap on my cold iron amulet warned me that one or more of them had just tried to hex me. Since Shakespeare didn't immediately burst into flames or otherwise die a gruesome death, I assumed his talisman protected him as well.

"Good night, now," I called cheerfully, just to let them know they'd failed, and we left them there to contemplate the profound disadvantages of summoning rituals. The risks are almost always greater than the reward.

Once we were well out of their sight and hearing, I paused to recover my cold iron talisman and place it back in my purse. Shakespeare helpfully remained unconscious until we returned to the stables and his feet touched ground. He was bleary-eyed and vomited again, much to the disgust of the stable boy, but rose gradually to lucidity as his synapses fired and memories returned.

"Marquis! You live! I live!" he said as I led him away to the White Hart, where I would gladly fall into bed in my room. His eyes dropped and he raised his hands and wiggled his fingers the way people do when they want to make sure that everything still works. "What happened?"

"What's the last thing you remember?"

"The witches—"

"Shh—keep your voice down!"

More quietly, he said, "The witches—they killed those men."

"Yes, they did. Is that all?"

His eyes drifted up for a moment, trying to access more details, but then dropped back down to me and he nodded. "That's the last thing I remember."

Fantastic! That was my cue to fabricate something. "Well, they threw the men in the cauldron, of course, while I threw you over my shoulder to sneak out of there."

"What? But what happened? Did they eat the men?"

"No, no, it was all divination, the blackest divination possible, powered by blood. They were asking Hecate to reveal the future for them."

"Zounds, God has surely preserved me from damnation. And you! Thank you sir, for my life. But what did they say?"

"I beg your pardon?"

"What matters did the hags seek to learn? The future of England?"

"I heard nothing beyond a general request to let the veil of time be withdrawn, that sort of thing. They were out of earshot before they got to specifics."

"But the chanting, before—you heard all of that, you translated some of it for me. What were their words, exactly—I need a quill and some ink!" He staggered into the White Hart Inn to find some, time of day be damned.

And that put me in the uncomfortable position of creating something that sounded like a spell but wasn't. I couldn't very well provide Shakespeare with the words one needed to summon Triple Hecate, knowing that he would immortalize them in ink.

So once he found his writing materials and demanded that I recount everything I could recall, providing a literal translation of the witches' chanting, I spun him some doggerel and he wrote it down: "Double, double, toil and trouble…"

And now you know why I shivered, Granuaile, when you said, "Fire burn and cauldron bubble."

Granuaile cried, "*You* wrote the witches' lines? No way!"

Shrugging and allowing myself a half grin, I said, "You're right. Shakespeare didn't write what I said into *Macbeth* verbatim. He played around with it a bit and made it fit his meter. Much better than what I said, to be sure. And the mystery of Hecate's summoning remained a mystery."

"The words alone wouldn't have been sufficient to do the deed, would they?"

"Not initially; I was worried about the cumulative effect. With such frequent invocation the goddess might have grown stronger and chosen to manifest at any time, with or without a sacrifice, and you don't want that version of Hecate to appear in a packed theatre."

Granuaile shook her head. "No, you don't. Why did they curse the play then?"

"Shakespeare never saw Hecate summoned but knew that the witches looked to her somehow, so she got written into *Macbeth*. The Hecate in his play is a single character and not particularly fearsome or strong. They thought his portrayal was demeaning and *that* inspired the curse."

"So they remained in England?"

"Long enough to see the play, yes. I don't think they realized that they had met the playwright in the past; they simply took grave offense and foolishly cursed it in concert within the hearing of others. They were caught and burned soon afterward."

<I'm kind of glad I didn't live in that time, Atticus,> Oberon said. <Over-boiled sausages are so disappointing. Dry and flavorless like kibble.>

That was your takeaway? Bad sausage at the White Hart Inn?

<Wasn't that the climax to your tragedy? Or was it the end where you and Shakespeare never even took a spoonful of what they were cooking in that cauldron?>

It wasn't a tragedy, Oberon. Nobody died except for those three guys and that was only because they were too stupid to leave us alone.

<Nobody ate anything delicious either so it sounded like a tragedy to me. I mean you had witches smeared with blood and fat so there had to be some meat cooking in there.>

It truly was a rough time. Luckily your circumstances are different. You got to eat what we cooked over the fire.

Oberon rolled over, presenting his belly, and stretched. <Yeah, I guess I have it pretty good. But shouldn't you be getting to work, Atticus? That belly isn't going to rub itself, you know.>

I obliged my hound and asked Granuaile if she felt like round two. She nodded and tossed me another beer from the cooler, grabbing one for herself. The pop and hiss of the cans sounded loud in the darkness, but after that it was only the occasional snap of the comfortably orange fire and the song that Gaia decided to sing to us under the unveiled stars.

Ashes

LAURA BICKLE

Blood sings.

It sings when the heart hammers too hard, when it rushes through lungs in a fury of breath, when it catches at the edge of a shout. It sings when the body yearns, when it fears, and when it chases. It divides the living from the dead.

Blood pounded in Anya Kalinczyk's ears as she ran, her soggy boots splashing through puddles. She bobbed and wove through a crowd of festival goers that seemed to be moving inexorably against her. Strains of music and shouting surrounded her as she fought to keep her target in sight: a squat, ragged figure scuttling behind legs and winding through the crowd like an eel. His right hand gleamed with flame, as if he was holding a torch. He trailed his hand along trash cans and cars, starting small blazes that guttered out in the fine March rain. Losing sight of her quarry, she ducked around the edge of a hot dog cart decked out in strobe lights to shout:

"Sparky! Which way did he go?"

A glowing shape slid around her legs and scuttled up the side of the nearest building: a five-foot long, mottled hellbender salamander. A writhing tongue slipped out from Sparky's teeth to scent the air. His head turned right, then left, then right again. His amber eyes seemed torn—torn between the weenie wagon and the crowd before them. And the strobe-lit hot dog cart was winning. His eyes dilated and he crept toward the hot dog cart advertising HOT FRESH DEVIL DOGS.

Anya sighed. *That's my familiar.*

Good thing that nobody but her could see him advancing upon the blinged-out weenie wagon. That would really bake the noodle of anyone who wasn't already shitfaced.

"Sparky," she barked. "The gnome. We need to find him."

Sparky looked down on her, giving her the dirtiest salamander look he could manage, with narrowed eyes and a head tilt that clearly communicated lack of respect for her priorities.

"You can visit the weenie wagon later. I swear. Just...find the gnome!"

Sparky huffed and scuttled along the building wall, top speed, tail lashing, ten feet up from the sidewalk. Anya struggled to keep up, finding a space of sidewalk occupied only by a tangle of duct-taped cords snaking away to carts, deep-fryers, and soundstage speakers. The sun had set, drawing shadows down on the street. Keeping one eye on the salamander, and the other on the treacherous footing, she followed him down the block. She tried very hard not to catalogue all of the fire code violations.

Sparky leaped neatly from building to building, old warehouses sporting crumbly bits of art deco corbels. He jumped from awnings to lintels and climbed along fractured brick, tracking their quarry with his preternatural senses. He could smell the dead much better than she could. A fire elemental was a born predator, and this one had a taste for ghost flesh.

A pair of young men stumbled across Anya's path. They reeked of beer, their devil masks pushed up high on their foreheads. One wore a sweatshirt with a graphic of a red imp on it that was lettered: DOWN WITH THE NAIN ROUGE.

"Dude…dude, did you see that?" The man in the sweatshirt grabbed the other's jacket and shook him.

The second man's head flopped forward like it was suspended on a rubber band. "That little red dude with the burning hand? Seriously pimped out…his eyes were red, man!"

Shit. Anya skidded to a stop before them. "Hey. That guy. Which way did he go?"

The guy with the sweatshirt blinked at her.

"The dude with the burning hand. Which way did he go?"

The man with the jacket pointed behind them. Sparky was on the case, turning the corner to an alley.

But shit was already going all pear-shaped. An overstuffed trash can was flaming out of control just ahead, the flames licking dangerously close to a funnel cake truck full of grease and pastries.

"That fucking imp," Anya growled. She snatched up a cooler of fluorescent sports drink and dumped the contents on the trash can. The fire fizzled out in a pop and hiss of orange sticky fluid.

"Hey!" a woman in an apron shouted. "That's my stuff."

Anya dug her badge out of her pocket. "Detroit Fire Department. This your truck?"

"Uhh, yeah." The woman squinted at the badge. "Are you a firefighter?"

"No, arson investigator. Someone set fire to your trash can…if I were you, I'd move it far away from your kitchen grease."

"Oh, my god." The funnel truck owner looked at the scorched mark on the side of her truck. In the middle of the scorch mark was a red handprint, tiny, like a child's. "Thank you. Who…did this?"

Anya bit her lip. There really wasn't any good way to explain who she was chasing. She briefly toyed with answering: "He's a supernatural primordial force that's tied to this area and is plenty pissed. He likes to set things on fire, and I'm looking forward to devouring his soul, because…what else do you do to something that keeps causing so much damage?"

Instead, she said: "Be on the lookout for a short red dude in a pimp coat."

"He's dressed like the Nain Rouge? Everybody around here is dressed like him." The woman spread her hand behind her, and her bracelets jingled. Half the crowd was in some sort of costume, from devil masks to pitchforks and pointy tails. It was sort of the point of a festival to drive out the ancient root of Detroit's evils, a harbinger of doom who'd been showing up at bloody scenes since the 1800s. He'd been a lurker since then, showing up at the sites of battles and disasters, making creeks run red and dancing on graves. The effort to exorcise him was symbolic, intended to create some solidarity and hope for the future.

But nobody was expecting the real Nain Rouge to turn up and start setting fire to shit. Anya hadn't either. She'd just expected that some dude dressed like him was a firebug causing her a headache. But she was beginning to believe that the Nain Rouge—the Red Dwarf of Detroit—might be real. And if he was real, that was gonna put her in a world of hurt.

"Just be careful, ma'am..."

A thump sounded above Anya, and she looked up to see an irritated salamander slapping his tail on the brick building towering above her. Thank God he was invisible to everyone else, since he was upside down and wiggling his gill fronds like a proper B-movie monster.

"I gotta find the guy. Excuse me." Anya pocketed her badge and followed Sparky to the corner of a building. The gap between two buildings created an alley, sticky with forgotten cotton candy and covered with cans and busted beer bottles. The noise from the crowd dropped away, and Anya had the sense of crossing a threshold, perhaps to her quarry's lair.

Sparky dropped down to the cracked asphalt floor of the alley, nose pressed to the ground. He led Anya to the corner of an empty warehouse. All the glass had been busted out of the windows, the remaining shards glinting like shiny teeth.

The door on the bottom was locked, but Sparky leapt nimbly up through a broken window. Anya shrugged out of her heavy leather jacket and cleared the glass teeth from the window frame with the sleeve. She hesitated, glimpsing a bloody handprint on the lintel.

She hauled herself up the sharply-cold metal, still coated with March frost. Her breath steamed before her as she gathered her bearings and plunged inside. She landed on her feet in a pile of trash, and automatically reached for her gun. Guns were of no use against a supernatural opponent. But she didn't know what else might be in that building.

Red light from the festival shone through the window frames in lurid light. She reached into her coat pocket for a flashlight. Sparky undulated forward in the dark, glowing a seething amber color, like a blind cave fish incandescing in deep cave water. She followed him across the sodden floor, up two flights of stairs to the top floor. Her light showed her a vast unpartitioned space that might have been a steno pool in an earlier time. The flashlight picked out the skeletons of typewriters and file cabinets, rusting under a steady drizzle of rain leaching in from the perforated roof.

And bloody tracks crossing the floor. They didn't look human… they looked like a giant bird's—three front toes and a wicked back claw. She followed the trail that seemed to travel with the rhythm of a human gait, around broken fans and rotting paper, until it suddenly stopped.

"Detroit Fire Department," she announced to the darkness. "Come on out with your hands up." *Even if they're burning.*

Laughter burbled somewhere above her. "I don't recognize your authority. A fire department is merely an illusion of elemental control." The voice that spoke sounded like the voice of a bird's—a raven taught to talk. The inflection was both gravelly and shrill. Inhuman.

"You're in a whole lotta trouble," she called. The more it talked, the more she could get a fix on it. She swept her flashlight beam above her. Water trickled down, screwing with her perception of movement. "Three arsons have been reported along the riverfront in the past week. Somebody blew up a city bus, set fire to an empty warehouse, and then decided to torch an armored bank truck. Which, I gotta tell you, was not successful. Who are you?"

A giggle emanated from her right, in the darkest part of the floor covered in debris. "I'm the Nain Rouge. The Red Dwarf. Bringer of darkness to a city that should never have been built."

Anya's light illuminated a figure perched on top of a ruined I-beam. The Nain Rouge clung to the metal with the legs of a giant bird. It seemed that his body was vaguely humanoid, though what she could see was flesh the red of old brick. He wore a tattered jacket of black feathers and a wizened face with red eyes stared back at her.

"Are you a ghost? Demon?"

The Nain Rouge shrugged, and the feathers on his coat rippled as if they'd sprung from skin. "I am eternal." He looked her up and down. "What are you?" he asked, cocking his head, as if he saw something shiny when he gazed at her.

"Fire Department," she responded, stubbornly. Anya was hoping she could pull off the idea of being a plain ordinary human long enough to get close to him, to take him down…

Sparky crept along the floor, his belly pressed to the puddles and litter. He stared up at the Nain Rouge, tail lashing. A low growl emanated from his throat.

"You have a fire salamander for a pet. And you smell like brimstone. Humans aren't supposed to smell like brimstone." He began to back away.

Awesome. Just awesome. Maybe she needed to change her deodorant. Anya slowly began to close on the dwarf. She holstered her gun to give the Nain Rouge a sense of false security. She opened her hands to show that she was harmless. "I just want to talk."

"You don't want to talk." The Nain Rouge squinted at her, perhaps seeing her in a magical light, as she truly was. "You're not even human. You're…I haven't seen what you are." Puzzlement twitched through the crags and valleys on his face as he tried to understand. "You're not a shaman…certainly nothing angelic…"

"I'm a Lantern," she whispered. She was the rarest type of medium. Where other mediums allowed spirits to use their hands and voices to communicate, Anya devoured them. It was helpful in her side job as a ghost hunter…and occasionally useful in her day job, in times, like now, when the supernatural crossed too far into the everyday world.

She reached for the dwarf. She had no hope of touching him with her hands, but she might be able to reach him with the inner fire that burned hungrily in her chest. That black hole in her energy field lashed out, searching for that spirit perched above her. She didn't know what kind of monster the imp was, but she knew that if she could pull it in, devour it, that it would be finished. She could sense the jagged edges of his terrible aura, feeling something ancient and wily, something strong and rooted in this place, like an ancient tree.

But the Nain Rouge was fast. He leaped from the beam into the darkness, scuttling overhead. Anya squinted into the dark, flinching as a dribble of water hit her in the face. Bits of the roof had fallen over time, and she struggled to distinguish the dwarf's shadow against the pinpricks of light from the sky.

"You can't escape," she said, sounding more certain than she felt. She'd consumed hundreds of ghosts, ripped them from the ether. This creature should be no different.

The Nain Rouge flitted away, and she gave chase. She spied the shadow crawling out through a bent metal door in the far wall, outlined with a crease of dim light from outside.

Anya straight-armed her way through the door, Sparky on her heels. She looked upward for the Nain Rouge, seeing grey sky and a flurry of feathers…

…and the floor fell out from beneath her with a shriek of metal.

She flailed, grasping for something, anything, and came up with a handful of groaning metal. Her legs dangled in space as she sucked in her breath. In counterpoint to her heartbeat, her copper salamander necklace pounded against her collarbone.

She'd burst out of the building onto a rusted fire escape… what was left of one. She clutched the remains of a railing, staring at the skeletal ruins of the fire escape falling a story below her. Pieces landed in the alley with deafening *clangs*.

"Sparky!"

The fire salamander was wound in the ladder above her, his feet wrapped around a sheared edge. The railing bent and groaned under Anya's weight. In her head, she ran through a dozen applicable fire code citations. Sparky leaned forward and grabbed the back of Anya's jacket in his mouth and began to haul her backward. The structure howled, and Anya heard screws popping out of the wall.

A hand reached out of the hole in the wall.

Without hesitation, Anya reached out to take it. Her left hand grasped her rescuer's arm as the right clutched the railing. The steel squealed and bent. Sparky leaped into the darkness of the door, and Anya let go of the metal. Her body slammed into the wall, and she was hauled into the doorway she'd fallen out of so unceremoniously.

Anya was dragged, panting, inside the dark doorway. Sparky licked her cheek.

"Fancy meeting you here."

Anya looked up. Her fingers were wound around the sleeve of a dark coat. The coat and the arm she clutched were attached to a blond man crouched over her. Dressed entirely in black, he looked as if he'd gotten lost in a record store in the 1980s and only recently had found his way out.

"Charon." She blinked, disentangling her fingers. "What in hell are you doing here?"

"Well, no. Not *in* Hell. And you're welcome."

"But, I mean…I've only seen you in the morgue. On this plane of reality, anyway. Doing the whole psychopomp thing. And you're looking awful corporeal, for this plane."

"I'm not bound there." He looked offended. "Besides, I'm still 'doing the psychopomp thing.' In between saving your ass. Are you hurt?" He lifted the dark curtain of her hair to inspect her face.

"No, I'm okay." Anya ducked away from his hand and sat up. She glanced at Sparky, who was busily gnawing one of Charon's boot laces. "Thanks, but…what are you doing here?"

"Same reason you're here, I suspect. Little short dude with a bad attitude?"

Sparky snorted.

"Not you," Charon amended, rubbing the salamander's nose. It annoyed Anya that Sparky was so comfortable with Charon, but she didn't really want to admit why it bothered her. "I'm here for the Nain Rouge."

"Hell wants the Nain Rouge?"

Charon rolled his eyes. "Hell's been trying to get him—and keep him—for years."

"Well, um, the underworld has had enough time to catch him, right? He's been running loose and creating havoc since before Detroit was a city."

"The boss thinks he's causing a bit too much havoc here, and drawing too much attention to the supernatural. I mean…" Charon rubbed his forehead. "…there's a goddamn festival here in his honor. Everybody dresses up as him, sings songs, and then burns him in effigy. It's like he's a rock star."

"The idea is to symbolically put the bad luck down for another year."

"Well, there is something to that. It's based on an old ritual that got lost as Detroit got more civilized. Doing it on the vernal equinox is great timing, and burning the little shit in effigy does drop him down in the underworld…for a little while. We chase him around. But he crawls right back out, no matter what we do."

"So they sent you this time?" Anya asked.

"They sent me. With something special to collar the imp." Charon opened his coat.

The interior of it glowed, and Anya's brow furrowed. "What *is* that?" As her eyes adjusted, she could make out a chain around Charon's waist. "New fashion statement?"

"Nope." Charon unwound the chain from his waist and wrapped it around his wrist. "This is Glepinir."

Anya wracked her brains for texts from her old mythology classes. "The chain that held Fenrir, the wolf in Norse mythology?"

"The one. It's used to bind Fenrir the wolf until the end of the world."

"Do I want to know what you're doing with Fenrir in the meantime?" She didn't want to contemplate Ragnorok falling down around their heads.

"Fenrir is having a slumber party with Kerberos. Left 'em at my house with a bag of kibble and a tube of tennis balls. Anyway," Charon shrugged, apparently unconcerned about the possibility of provoking the apocalypse by literally letting loose the dogs of war. He showed her the end of the chain, which had been fashioned into a collar-like lasso. "I'm thinking Glepinir will work on the Nain Rouge because it was wrought by dwarves. Totally unbreakable."

Sparky looked at the leash and hissed, the gill fronds on the sides of his head extending in fear.

Anya threw her arms around the salamander. "Nobody's going to put a leash on you."

"Did you bring any of your fellow ghost hunters for reinforcement on this case, or is it just you and the salamander?"

Anya shook her head. “Nope. Just me and the giant amphibian.”

“You got kicked out.” He said it with a bit of smugness that irritated her.

“No. Look, the group has been under a lot of stress lately. With the death of Ciro, and…” she trailed off. Things had been really bad. The last run they’d gone on, nobody had bothered to call her. She didn’t want to admit how much that had hurt. Not to herself, and especially not to Charon.

“Uh-huh. Well, you know I don’t like your boyfriend.”

Anya rolled her eyes and bit back a snide retort. Her love life was none of the psychopomp’s business, but it still stung. “Yeah, well. He’s not been around much.”

“Good. Mortals just get in the way.” Charon stood up, tugging his sleeve over the glittering leash.

Anya bristled as she hauled herself to her feet. “I take offense at that.”

Making a dismissive gesture, he turned toward the less-painful exit of the building. “You don’t count.”

“Why the hell not?”

Looking over his shoulder, Charon grimaced. “Oh, come on. Your dad—” He cut himself off and shook his head.

“Hey. What about my dad?”

“Never mind. Let’s just get the gnome, and then we can have a talk over coffee or the spirit of your choice.”

She caught his sleeve and turned him around to face her. “You can’t just dangle clues like that at me.”

He sighed. “Look, that’s not my story to tell.”

Grabbing his collar, she hauled his face down to her level. "Tell me, or I'm not helping you."

He snorted. "You're not gonna let that gnome roam free. You have a conscience."

She jerked his collar, and Sparky began to chew on the hem of his coat. "You're still a ghost on this plane, okay? Which means you're supper for the salamander and a case of indigestion for me. Spill it."

He looked at her with resignation. "Your dad is a phoenix."

She released him and rocked back on her heels. "What the hell?"

"Well, he visits Hell from time to time." He pinched the bridge of his nose. "Ah, piss. He's gonna kill me."

Anya punched him in the arm. "You know my dad and you didn't tell me?"

"Look, I thought you *knew*. Or didn't want to know. Or were avoiding the whole thing. Or something."

"My dad is a phoenix?" she repeated. "How in the hell does that work?"

"He's like…the king of fire elementals. He doesn't really have a fixed form. He's the embodiment of flame, and he can shift into pretty much whatever shape he wants. Can we get back to work now? Please?" Not looking back to see if she followed, he strode briskly away.

Anya looked down at Sparky. "Did you know?"

Sparky gazed up at her solemnly, with big liquid eyes. And blew her raspberries.

"As they say, the dead travel fast."

Charon kicked at a burning piece of caramel-colored goo. It stuck to his boot, and he tried to shake it off. He doused his boot in a puddle.

"Yeah." Anya crossed her arms and gazed at the tower of burning caramel popcorn. It rose in an impressive plume of orange flame, like the special effects at a rock show. The vendor's booth that had held hundreds of bags of popcorn had gone up in a tower of blistering fire that reached beyond the streetlights.

"You, um, gonna do something to put that out?" Charon scraped his boot on the curb.

"Nope. Bystanders are all clear. Popcorn burns like Styrofoam. It's gonna go out by itself in about…now."

The flare collapsed in black smoke and guttered under the patter of a soft spring rain.

Anya nodded. "And now…the smell."

The acrid smell of burned popcorn and scorched sugar wafted over them as the wind changed direction. Charon rubbed his nose. "Gah. It smells like the fifth circle of Hell."

"The fifth circle? Isn't that anger?"

"Yeah."

"I woulda thought that the third circle would smell like popcorn. Gluttony, and all."

"Nah. Wrath smells just like this. Especially nineteenth-century wrath, for some weird reason I haven't figured out yet."

Anya approached the burnt out and stinking popcorn vendor's stall. The damn dwarf was playing with them now. She chewed her bottom lip, poking through the burnt and stinking mess with a piece of debris.

Something glinted, catching her attention. A rivulet of red liquid ran from the scorch mark on the pavement. She followed it, to where it ran into the gutter of the street. The gutter ran red with blood. Sparky snooted at it and twitched his gill fronds, disgusted.

"Shit," she said.

"Niiiice." Charon squinted at the crimson. "The Red Dwarf likes red."

"Yeah. After the Battle of Bloody Run in 1763, Parents' Creek ran red with blood. Pontiac's Rebellion was well underway, and the British attempted a sneak attack from Fort Detroit."

"Didn't go well for the British."

"No. And—*GAH!*" Anya shrieked as a sheet of cold water doused her.

Charon gazed sourly over his shoulder at a group of people in Detroit Fire Department slickers, busily dousing the smoking wreck of the popcorn stand with a fire hose. His hair dripped over his face, and he shoved it back with his palm.

Sparky growled, shaking himself off like a dog.

"Sorry, ma'am!" A rookie wrestling with the hose waved at her.

Anya flung water off her hands, futilely. She was soaked and freezing. And pissed.

"You could shut the festival down," Charon said. As he walked forward, his boots squeaked.

"That's what he wants," she said. "We have to catch him."

"What if he hurts someone?"

Anya briskly began to follow the receding trail of blood downhill. "I intend to take him down permanently—since it sounds like Hell can keep track of him." She gritted her teeth. "He's the prime supernatural source of misfortune here in Detroit. Would I sacrifice a popcorn stand or a bus or two to put him down permanently? I have to think…yes?"

"I dunno. It's a no-brainer for me. You're the one saddled with human morals. I'm just reminding you of them."

Giving him a dirty look, she stalked down the street, shivering, following the diluted red as it slinked away. She tracked it down the street as it sloped toward the river, dodging costumed festival-goers as she worked. It bothered her that she hadn't called up the police department and disbursed the festival as a kneejerk reaction. It bothered her that her calculus was this cold, that she was willing risk harm for the chance to nail the gnome.

But she believed. Or, she wanted to, as she looked up at the darkening skyline of her city. She wanted to believe that all Detroit's ills could be blamed on this one thing, and that this was something she could do something about. She couldn't do anything much about economic disaster, unemployment, or street crime. But she could fix this.

In the twilit distance, the parade was assembling. St. Ann's Church stood at the end of the street, illuminated in bright light. Flags, balloons, and glow sticks waved before the start of the parade route, the march that would go downhill to the river, where an effigy of the Nain Rouge would be burned. The effigy itself stood before the church on a long pole, made of straw and papier-mâché, looking like a Halloween caricature of a devil. She estimated that there were a couple of hours left before the effigy was burned…and dropped the Nain down to Hell, temporarily. She didn't look forward to chasing the little shit around the underworld.

The red trail dripped away to a storm drain in the street. She squatted beside it, disappointed. The red slipped down between the iron spaces in the grate, leading nowhere.

"Damn it," she grumbled.

But something was moving below the grate. She put her face down close to the grate and squinted. Sparky pressed his snout to the grate and pawed at it.

Charon stood over them. "You think he went down there?"

"Something's down there. Sparky's got the scent of a ghost." Anya whistled for the fire crew and flashed her badge.

The rookie on the hose crew looked abashed as she showed her badge to him. "I'm really sorry…"

"Never mind that. Can you get this grate up?"

"Uhhh…sure. Why?"

"Inspection. I think there's something flammable down there." Which wasn't that far from the truth.

"Um, okay." He trotted back to the fire truck and conferred with the other members of the crew. A man in a yellow rain slicker came back with a hydraulic rescue tool. As he wedged the tool under the edge of the grate, the other men lifted. The sewer grate came up easily, exposing a two foot by three foot chasm in the street. The crew began cordoning off the hole with caution tape.

"Thanks, guys," she said.

The rookie, an apologetic look all over his baby face, handed her a yellow rain slicker. "Are you going down there alone?"

Anya glanced at Charon and Sparky. They were real and solid to her, but she kept forgetting that they were invisible to regular people…what Charon had called "mere mortals."

"Yeah. I'll be back soon."

She shone her flashlight down the hole. There was no sign of movement now, but she wasn't surprised that the racket had driven the Nain Rouge off. At least, with him underground, there was less chance of him wreaking havoc at street level. Maybe.

Sparky plunged into the dark, tail churning. His feet gripped the bricked side of the storm sewer and he vanished from view. Charon swung down after him. The underworld was his territory, and he slid down the outside rungs of the access ladder like a fireman coming home.

"Sparky!" she hissed, fumbling with the metal rungs. Her boots slipped on the edges, and she had to go slowly to keep her balance. The last step was a doozy, and she jumped off into a knee deep puddle of frigid storm water.

It's just storm water, she told herself as a flotilla of beer cans and Styrofoam cups drifted past her knees. Just storm water. Not sewer water.

"I don't see your salamander." Charon was holding his right hand, wrapped with the glowing Glepinir, up as a light.

"Sparky!" she called, scanning the ripples of the black water with her flashlight.

She thought she spied a splash, then a ripple, but then there was nothing.

"Sparky!"

Slogging in the freezing water, she reached the ripple. But it was just water flowing around a piece of broken concrete. Staring up at the brick wall, she saw a smear of blood…a smear in the shape of a salamander foot.

"If that son of a bitch hurt Sparky…" Tears glazed her eyes. Sparky had never failed to come when called. She was willing to contemplate the Nain Rouge causing harm to strangers, risking the unknown on this mission, but she would not risk Sparky. Not ever.

Charon was at her elbow, his sodden coat trailing in the water. "Sparky's a tough critter."

"I'm gonna devour that bastard. I'm gonna tear that bastard to pieces and enjoy every bit…"

She charged forward, downstream, toward the river. She figured that the Nain Rouge would try to intercept the effigy before it was burnt at the edge of the river. She could be wrong…he could be heading upstream toward the church. Hesitating, she was just about to tell Charon to divide their forces, when she spied a silhouette in her flashlight beam just ahead.

"Hey!"

She ran to it, the water sliding coldly down her boots.

The dark shadow turned away from her and began to flee.

A glowing tongue of light flashed out from behind Anya. *Glepinir*, she realized. The golden chain lashed out and caught the figure, like a cowboy lasso around an errant calf. The silhouette collapsed in the water. Charon began hauling it in.

"You're like Wonder Woman," Anya panted.

"Strength. Beauty. Wisdom. I do what I can."

Anya reached down in the water for the figure. To her disappointment, it was not the Nain Rouge. But it was still pretty dead.

Anya hauled the man up by his dripping lapels. Glepinir was wrapped around his elbows and neck. He was dressed in a colonial blue uniform, with a pasty pale young man's face under dark hair. His chest was completely torn open, and there was an empty cavity where his heart should have been.

"What did you do with my salamander?" she snarled, her knee in his ruined chest.

"N-nothing! I did nothing to your creature!" He spoke in a British accent, and his breath smelled like a butcher shop.

"Tell me where the salamander is!" Anya pressed her hand to his face. She could feel the terrible vacuum in her chest opening. She'd relish devouring this ghost, if he'd hurt Sparky…

The ghost gasped. "I don't know! The…the little dragon was chasing the Nain Rouge!"

Anya felt Charon's hand on her shoulder, and she drew back.

"Who are you?" the psychopomp asked.

"Captain James Dalyell, of the Queen's Army, First Regiment, Aide-de-Camp to General Jeffrey Amherst…"

"What are you doing here?" Anya demanded. This could be a touchy question. Some ghosts had no self-awareness and had no idea why they haunted the places they did. Pressing them could cause a meltdown. Normally, she'd ease a ghost into existential questions, but she was in no mood to be gentle.

"I've been here…" His brow wrinkled. "Since the battle… when the creek ran red."

"You've been here since the Battle of Bloody Run?" Charon squatted down on his heels, squinting at the ghost.

"Yes." Dalyell's fingers trailed to his chest, and his eyes glazed. "I led the attack, and…Pontiac took my heart. Last thing I remember as a living man is seeing my blood smeared on the faces of my men…" His vision cleared, and he looked sharply at Charon, then Anya. "And true death has finally come for me at last. Please, take me."

"Do you know where the Nain Rouge is?" Anya interrupted.

"Yes. The monster. He came to my tent and whispered into my ear to lead the charge…He promised me victory and glory, and I am ashamed to say that I listened to him." Dalyell turned away, and the shame still glowed in his face. "He danced on the shore of the creek as my men were slaughtered." His hands balled into fists. "I would see him dead…ah, *more* dead. I have chased him for centuries, but I have not succeeded. He is too strong for me. All I can do is watch." His head hung forward in centuries-old shame.

"Will you lead us to him if we promise to destroy him?"

"And will you grant me eternal rest?"

Anya frowned. She had no idea what happened to the spirits she devoured, if they simply stopped existing, or if they went someplace else entirely. To heaven? To Charon's underworld? This wasn't a promise that she could make.

"Yes," Charon said, with some authority. Anya shot him a sidelong glance.

"I'd be honored to contribute to that imp's demise. But you'll need to free me, first." Dalyell shrugged against Glepinir.

Charon slipped the lasso back over Dalyell's head to release him. Anya half-expected the ghost to vanish—spirits were often treacherous—but he stayed in corporeal form.

Dalyell slogged to his feet. "This way. The imp has many hiding places, but his favorite is near the river. I believe it feeds his power, and that he must return to it often to replenish himself."

Anya fell into step behind him, Charon at her elbow. Her teeth chattered in her head, and she wrapped the yellow fireman's coat tightly about her.

"You should change jobs, you know," Charon said. "Blow this popsicle stand. Consider working with me."

"As an errand-girl for Hades?" Her flashlight beam jounced over the water and the walls in time with her shivering. She admitted to herself that the underworld would be warmer.

"It beats your current digs. Hell has benefits. Full medical and dental for you and the salamander. Plus commission."

"What commission are you getting for bringing the Nain Rouge in? More chow for the hellhound? New sulfurous hot tub?"

"A soul. One in particular." He smirked.

Anya shivered, deep down in the molten void inside her chest.

Dalyell led them through the underground tunnels of the storm sewer. He seemed mindful to pick the shallower water for Anya's sake, but it seemed that the water continued to rise, sluicing through grates above. Anya could hear the staccato rhythm of rain on the pavement above and the marching of feet. Music and bits of laughter, popping balloons and joyous shrieks trickled down. The parade was underway.

"We have to find him before they light the effigy," Charon groused. "I won't be able to find him in Hell…these tunnels are a hamster habitat compared to all the places he can hide in the underworld."

Dalyell glanced back at him. "You mean to bring him to Hell for good?"

"That's my aim." Charon stabbed a thumb at Anya. "She wants to eat him for dinner."

The British captain gazed at her with narrowed eyes. "This mission makes for strange bedfellows."

Anya changed the subject. "Do you think that taking out the Nain Rouge would remove the…the misfortune from Detroit?"

Dalyell drummed his fingers on his empty chest. "I believe that it would. The Nain Rouge is more ancient than any people, white or copper, on this land. I have come to believe that he is a force of nature…never human. I watched him climb up into the light to harass the people before the Great Fire."

"The Great Fire of 1805?" Anya asked, brow wrinkling.

"Yes. I believe that he set it, that he chose his time and place and burned the city down. I believe that he is tied to the land, and that once that tie is broken, that the land would be wholly free to seek its own destiny, for good or for ill." The light was growing grey at the end of the tunnel, illuminating fragments of faded graffiti on the cement walls. Anya heard the sound of water rushing.

Dalyell pointed. "Look!"

The round storm drain tunnel opened out into a spillway along the banks of the river. Red water coursed swiftly around Anya's ankles, and she struggled to keep her balance. Before her, the black water of the river reflected night, spangled with rain. To her right, she dimly registered the bridge spanning the river, headlights washing up and away into the darkness.

"Sparky!" she shouted.

In the shallows, Sparky was attacking the gnome. He'd climbed up on the gnome's back and was snapping at his neck. Flailing and hissing, the Nain Rouge tried to reach back to attack the salamander. Sparky's tail lashed right and left, and blood speckled his coppery hide.

Anya plunged into the frigid water after her dear salamander. The Nain Rouge ripped the salamander off his back and flung him to the rocks piercing the shallow water. Sparky made a piteous squeak when he struck, twitching.

"Sparky," Anya breathed. She hauled the salamander's body to her chest, cradling him, ignoring the gnome splashing away in the river.

Sparky curled his tail around her waist and buried his head under her coat, next to her heart. Running her fingers over his skin, she inspected him for injuries. He was soaked and sticky with blood; there was no way of telling how much of it was his and how much of it was the gnome's. He was a supernatural entity, to be certain…but he could be hurt by supernatural things. Even killed.

"Oh, Sparky. I'm sorry."

She stroked his gill fronds, and he rewarded her with a lick on the side of her cheek.

She glanced back over her shoulder with a murderous glare. Where was that goddamn imp?

The Nain Rouge was swimming in the river, cutting into the blackened water like an eel. Charon had gone after him. The psychopomp's sodden coat remained behind on the bank in a heap, and she could make out his bright blond hair bobbing in the water, glowing in the light of Glepinir slung around his shoulders. Like the tentacles of a jellyfish in tropical water, the tendrils of the magic leash drifted behind Charon.

Behind and above her, she could see the glow of the parade and hear chanting and singing at street level. The straw effigy of the Nain Rouge bobbed along on a pole, looking like a scarecrow with a plastic devil's mask taped on it. Torches were coming, a block distant, zigging and zagging like sparks from a bonfire. She knew they'd been lit in the purifying flames of St. Anne's candles, and they were coming for the effigy.

"*Burn…burn…burn…*" the crowd chanted.

"No time!" she screamed at Charon.

The imp was making toward one of the bridge supports. He scrambled out of the water as nimbly as a frog and clambered up the support with his wicked talons. His right hand was burning like the torches behind her, only more intensely…it was white hot. It fizzled in the rain, leaving red marks on the bridge supports.

How hot was he burning? He had to be burning at three thousand degrees to burn the metal like that. Rain sizzled and evaporated in a halo around him.

Charon burst out of the water at the base of the bridge. Glepinir glowed in his grip, and he flung the noose at the monster.

The leash caught around the Nain Rouge's burning arm, flaring as bright as a star. The imp pulled back, hard. It was a terrible tug of war, the unbreakable links of Glepinir caught around the fist of the monster and the ferryman of the dead.

It was in that moment that Anya realized how strong that the Nain Rouge really was. He wasn't an annoyance or a joke. He was an elemental force, like gravity or light or magnetism, a creature of earth and power far beyond her estimation.

Anya turned to Dalyell. "Take him." She pressed the salamander into Dalyell's arms, wrapped in her yellow fireman's coat. She stripped off her jacket and plunged into the water.

The water was shockingly cold, driving the breath from her. She wondered how Charon had stood it. Well, he wasn't human… she gritted her teeth and drew forward into the black cold, searching for the gold light of Glepinir.

Charon was swearing, and not just in English. Anya recognized English, Polish, and a dusting of Russian before he devolved into Latin and a smattering of Aramaic. In the treacherous sliver of footing he had claimed at the tower foundation, he was holding Glepinir wrapped around both fists. Yet the gnome was dragging him forward.

She clawed up to the concrete support of the bridge tower. She staggered to her feet to reach up and help Charon. Wrapping her fingers around the leash above his, she could feel the fine chain burning under the stress of the battle. Rain sizzled where it made contact with the links.

"What is he made of?" she choked. But she knew the answer: evil. Pure evil.

Charon's voice was in her ear: "Go get him."

Anya stared up at the feathered form of the Nain Rouge, clinging to the support tower. Holding Glepinir as tight as she could, she reached up for the cross-cut struts. She put one hand before another on the rain-slick rusted metal, climbing with numb feet. She had to get within range of the demon, devour him before Charon weakened.

A horrible creaking sound emanated from above, the shriek of metal. In horror, she looked up to see that the Nain Rouge was burning…all of him, as if he were the effigy. Where he clung to the bridge tower, the metal was melting and buckling. A fissure formed in the floor of the bridge, and a chunk of pavement tore and rolled into the water with a shearing sound.

Anya was momentarily bathed in headlights as a speeding truck hit the fragmented pavement. Dimly, she realized that it was a fuel truck. Brakes squealed, and the truck sawed right and left, out of control. It hit the guardrail, shattering the metal, slid over the edge. The cab plunged forward while the stainless steel tanker skidded and sparked on the ledge. A plume of fire traced along its seams as it careened into the shallows of the river with a deafening crush of metal and rock.

It hit with a force that nearly jolted Anya from her precarious perch—she felt it in the back of her dental fillings. Fire raced along the river surface, over the half-submerged tank, blossoming along the spreading gasoline.

The river was red, red and burning.

The Nain Rouge bellowed a victorious roar into the red rain.

And Glepinir snapped.

The mighty leash broke. Anya ducked against the vibrating support beam. The edge of the leash lashed away.

The cable whipped back at Charon, slashing him in the chest. He stumbled back, a great bloom of red crossing his chest, and fell back in the burning water.

Anya looked up. The Nain Rouge swung the remains of Glepinir over his head and began to dance, his bird-claw feet twitching on the support tower.

"No. No you don't. I won't let you."

Anya scrambled the last three yards to the Nain Rouge. She reached up for him, grabbing his burning feathers and opening the terrible hole in her chest. She wrapped her arms around him as he tried to cling to the support.

She pressed her cheek to his filthy face, and her skin sizzled. *"You will come with me."*

Her fingers dug into his feathers, into his flesh, as the fire within her chest reached out to devour him. Her aura winged out in an amber glow, suffusing the gnome's burning.

He fought her. Struggling in her arms, she could feel his spirit twitching and fighting her. He had a huge, vast soul… much larger than she had ever tried to consume before. It was as if he was a spirit of place, the *genius loci*, a tremendous force. She could feel his misery and his ache, the torment he left behind. Behind her eyes, she saw him dancing on the river bank, dancing in victory as the city burned, yesterday, today, and tomorrow.

It hurt. God damn it, it hurt. Tears leaked from her eyes, and she whispered: "*Come dance with me, you son of a bitch.*"

As she took another breath to draw the life force from him, his grip slackened. He let go…

…and there was nothing but darkness and light and the prickle of rain against her face as they pitched into space. Still, she held on. She locked her arms around him as they fell, together. She breathed him in, fed on him, on all that terrible life force that had animated him through the centuries. She held on even when they passed through the fire and struck the water with terrible force. Bones crackled, but she held on.

She held on as they sank below the surface of the water, the fire and red light above them, through the heat and the frigid cold. Sucking all the life from him into her glowing chest, she choked on the ancient evil of it. Her lungs burned as she inhaled; whether it was his soul or the water didn't matter—it was all a part of him, and she was determined to kill him.

He kicked and struggled, but she locked her arms together. And he struggled less, and less. She opened her mouth, could see the terrible red light leaking from her lips. She could feel his life force splitting her skin open. She burned, drawing the last of the life from this evil, maleficent vessel.

She touched bottom with her shoulder, something sharp. The Nain Rouge was still in her grip, empty. His head sagged forward, and his arms floated up like pool noodles. It seemed that he shriveled in her arms, like a garbage bag drained of air.

She lifted her head. The light above was too far.

Her eyes began to drift closed.

But she saw something before her. Glowing eyes. Not just one set, many…

She closed her eyes.

"Let go."

She opened her eyes.

Charon was standing over her. At least, she thought it was Charon. He looked different. He looked mostly like himself, but he was surrounded by an oddly black aura, soft as raven feathers. His chest was oozing blood, but he was still as waterlogged, as if he'd climbed out of a river.

She tried to speak, but couldn't. Her throat was swollen, and everything hurt. More than it should be allowed to hurt.

Something cool slid across her cheek, purring against her skull. Sparky. His tongue washed away her tears and came back red with blood. He pressed his nose to her chin and whimpered.

"Let go, darling," Charon said again. And she realized that she was still holding the Nain Rouge, or what was left of him. Her arms were still embracing a pile of blackened bones and ash that smoked.

Charon gently pulled her arms away from the mass. She would have screamed if she could have, but she had nothing left to scream with. After tossing away the Nain Rouge's shell, Charon knelt beside her on one side. Sparky snuggled on her other. In the distance, she was conscious of fire sirens, of the sounds of revelry on the street above. She tipped her head a fraction of an inch, and she could see the glare of something burning silhouetted against the sky. The effigy. They must be on the river bank, near the sewer.

"They burned the effigy. But you did it." Dalyell peered at her over Sparky. His chest was smooth and unmarked; she realized that his heart had been restored to him. "You saved the city. Thank you."

Reaching out to touch her shoulder, he smiled at her, a brilliant smile. And faded away, like frost melting.

Anya glanced back at Charon. She still couldn't move. She didn't know if that was from the cold, but she was suspecting that it was worse. Much worse.

"I'm giving you a decision to make," Charon said, smoothing a lock of singed hair from her face. The lock broke off and landed on her cheek. "You have to decide to stay or to go."

Her brows drew together as she looked down at her body. Her skin was raw and blackened; she knew she'd been horribly burned. Her body felt swollen, like a charred marshmallow. Bits of light leaked out from the webbing between her fingers and lacerations on her arms. She couldn't imagine what the rest of her body looked like. The Nain Rouge had been too strong for her.

She looked up at Charon sharply. *He* was giving her a decision? He knelt above her, darkly incandescing, all pretenses lost. "Look, I haven't been straight with you. I'm not just a psychopomp. I'm… Death." He pressed his hand to her forehead. "You can choose to come with me, or to stay."

She narrowed her eyes at him. She dredged up her voice, which felt like a drain cleaner on her throat and came out as the merest whisper: "Is the city safe?"

Charon looked up at the flaming horizon, at the red river. "The slate is clean. With the Nain Rouge gone, its destiny is entirely within its own hands, for good or ill."

She sighed.

"I'll be honest, your physical body is pretty fucked up. If you choose to stay, you'll have a short road ahead of you before I see you again." He folded her fingers in his and kissed the black fingertips. "If you come back with me, I'll give you a job. Bounty hunter. Reaper. Princess of Hell, whatever you like. And I'll introduce you to your dad."

Her breath snagged in her throat. She glanced at Sparky through charred eyelashes.

"The salamander goes where you go. Even I couldn't change that."

She stared up at the sky, at the raindrops coming down from above. She'd worked invisibly for the city, had done her best. She thought of the ghost hunting group that she loved dearly, the team that was collapsing under the stress of death and loss. She thought of her lonely work as an arson investigator, always on the outside looking in. She thought of her friends, of Katie and Marsh. She thought of Brian, who grew ever more distant each day, as if he was a man slowly becoming one with his machines.

Her eyes burned. She belonged here. Didn't she? Now, she only knew that she was tired. Tired. Disconnected. Extinguished. She just wanted to be someplace that she would be...understood. Accepted. Maybe even loved.

Her blood sang at the thought.

Charon said. "Come home."

She exhaled. "Okay."

He kissed her forehead. "Let go."

She was afraid if she closed her eyes, there would be interminable darkness that she would never claw her way free of, that she would become a dimmer version of herself or be smothered entirely.

But there was a spark. And then a fire.

It washed over her in an orange sheet. The fire burned away the cold and the pain in a soft roar. It sank deep within her bones, quickening her blood. Her blood sang within her, reaching deep inside the dark hollow of her chest and filling it with liquid warmth. She felt her bones reknit, her flesh stretching supplely over warm muscle. She felt as if she'd sunk beneath the surface of a hot bathtub for hours with an unlimited supply of hot water.

She felt alive. Whole, for perhaps the first time, as the cool drizzle caressed her skin.

Her breath steamed in front of her in the dark March night. She climbed to her feet in a pile of ash. Ash covered her from neck to toe, but the luxurious warmth remained. Embers glowed at her feet, with the heat of warm stones, dispersing into the dark like fireflies. As the ash blew away, she saw the glimmer of copper armor covering her skin. Her hair fell forward against her face, warm as a towel from the dryer. She looked down at her hands. They were grubby, but whole. Reaching up for her neck, she was relieved to feel that her copper salamander torque had survived the fire.

Sparky wound around her ankles, trilling. His toes flexed in the scorched earth around her, growing filthy in carbon black.

Looking back, she saw the crumpled remains of the Nain Rouge's body. She steeled herself to see some shell of her body lying on the ground beside him, that she was now wearing her soul, forever divided from it.

But there was nothing but ash and burning silt. Behind her, the river still burned, throwing smoke in the air in great plumes. Her firefighter's coat and Charon's coat were crumpled on the bank, but that was all that remained. No bones. No bodies. No evidence that she ever was.

Charon stood before her. He had dropped the glamour he'd always shown her before—or maybe she was just now seeing him clearly. He was dressed in black, his black aura curling around him. The Flock of Seagulls hair had collapsed in the downpour, and it seemed that he wore a sense of shocked gravitas that she hadn't sensed before.

His brow knitted as he extended a hand to her. "Well, that complicates things."

She reached forward and took his hand, inhaling deeply. Her lungs felt whole and unscarred, not scraped and bruised, like she usually did after devouring a spirit. "What?"

"You're the daughter of a phoenix." He regarded her as if she was wholly impossible.

"So you said." Lifting her head, she regarded the glowing skyline. She felt pretty damn alive. She expected that death would feel…floaty? Numb? Gauzy? "This feels pretty good for dead."

He laughed. "I suspect you're always going to be beyond my reach."

She lifted her eyebrows. Perhaps that wasn't a bad thing.

"You promised me that you'd take me to my father."

"Look."

He pointed up at the sky. A streak of fire sliced through the night, looking like a meteor. Anya squinted. She thought she detected the shape of wings before it faded from view in the afterglow of the city light. Sparky stood up on his back legs and craned his neck, the glimmer reflected in his eyes.

"Let's go home," Charon said. "I've got a feeling that he'll show up."

He led her back the way they'd come, to the mouth of the storm drain. Deep within, she could see a warm orange glow that hadn't been there before, the welcoming shine of a fire. In the distance, she heard barking. Kerberos and Fenrir, no doubt. Sparky splashed ahead, trilling in greeting.

She grinned. For the first time in a long time, she was full of anticipation. Full of life. Hopeful.

Charon cupped her filthy face in his hands, searching her face with his blue eyes. His dipped his head and kissed her. He tasted like fire and light, like something she'd been missing in that vast chasm of her empty chest.

Blood sings.

The Death of Aiguillon

ALIETTE DE BODARD

In the end, as she had known she would, Huyen crept back to the House of Aiguillon.

Dawn was barely breaking over Paris: a sick, vague pink tinge to the maelstrom of spells that filled the entire sky like roiling clouds. No sun, no stars; merely the acrid taste of spent magic that settled in the lungs like the beginnings of a cough, and a haze over the cobblestones that could hide anything from explosives to chimeras.

The great gates hung open. Through the haze, Huyen caught a glimpse of bodies, lying like discarded puppets in the gardens; and of what had once been the corridors, now open to the winds, with the familiar peony wallpaper singed and torn—Huyen remembered running with one hand following the flowers, drawing a line through the corridor as a way to find her way back to the kitchens—another time, another age. The House had succumbed, and nothing would ever be the same.

The soldiers were gone, leaving only the scavengers: the Houseless and the poor, hacking at hands, tearing fine clothes in their haste to take something, anything that would be of use to them.

She was Houseless now. She needed the clothes, and the jewellery, as much as the thin, grimy men and women. But—

But they were her dead; the faces she'd laughed with, smiled at, bowed to. Huyen took a deep, trembling breath, and crept closer into the gardens.

It was fine. It would be fine. If she could find a ring or a necklace; or an artefact charged with Fallen breath or fingernails: something, anything of value…

The first body she saw was swarmed over by two boys, who gave her a wary grin, but didn't discourage her as she crept closer. Nothing much there; not even a face—but the second one, pale and dishevelled and with purple lips—the second one was Valerie, one of the pantry girls, with a hole in her innards and a missing hand, and eyes bulging out of their sockets.

Heaven, she was going to be sick. She was going to…No, no weakness. She could not afford to show it, not in the middle of other predators. It was each for themselves now; and the boys still staring at her would not hesitate to hack at her own fingers if they thought there was value in it.

Each for themselves.

Huyen forced herself to walk, one tottering step at a time: past the bodies, past the arbour where she'd read the books she borrowed from the House's library. Past the ruined gates; and into the corridors now exposed to wind and rain. Overhead, the sky was still roiling with dark clouds; the air charged with dust that burnt her lungs.

Somehow, wandering through the desolation, she found herself in the kitchens—unrecognisable now, the walls marked with the sooty imprint of bodies caught in fire-spells; the water in the sink dark with blood; the pantry holding only crumbs and the sickening smell of burnt flesh. No bodies there—that made it worse, in a way; unreal; as if the destruction and death were just a tactical exercise, a dream she'd wake up from if she pinched herself hard enough.

But it was real. It was her life now; and if she didn't remember that she would be no better than the corpses littering the gardens.

Something caught her eye, at the back of the room: a flash of colour like a scrap of cloth. Something that hadn't been scavenged by others: a blanket or a tapestry or a cloak?

There was nothing when she got there, though; just the empty furnaces, with traces of soot—and then a hand shot out, catching hers in an unbreakable grip.

What—a soldier. There hadn't been someone there—she tried to free herself, frantically, but the hand wouldn't let go—*what an idiot…*

And then she looked up; and she knew the face.

It was gaunt, and scarred; and covered in dust, the eyes two pinpoints of burning ice; but still, there was a fraction of the old, effortless grace. "Mandias," she whispered.

He was Fallen, a minor one in the House's hierarchy; a helper in the alchemist's laboratory—but still far, far above her, someone she wouldn't be allowed to look at, let alone speak to. He was still young, as Fallen went; his skin faintly radiant with the memory of the Fall, his movements smooth, the shoulders bunching up as if he still remembered what it had been like to fly in the City of Heaven.

Mandias watched her, warily. "Heloise," he said.

Huyen hadn't expected him to remember her name. "It's Huyen now," she said. If she was going to be Houseless and destitute in Paris, she might as well take back the name Mother had given her, reclaim the familiar cadences of the language she hadn't spoken in decades.

"Huyen." His voice was smooth, faultless. Most Frenchmen couldn't hit the right tone on her name, but he did it surprisingly, effortlessly. "I didn't think—how did you survive?"

Because she'd hid and fled, when the doors burst. Because—she shook herself, forced herself to think. This wasn't time for gossip or chitchat: as Eugenie said, you couldn't trust one of the upper crust to have their heads screwed on right. "We have to leave," she said.

Mandias's grip on her didn't lessen. She could feel the heat of his magic roiling through the skin, like a trapped wildfire. "The soldiers—"

Huyen closed her eyes: seeing, again, the nightmare of uniformed men swarming over familiar places; the head cook, Frederic, standing in their path for a bare moment before his chest exploded in a shower of blood; and the kitchen staff scattering, rushing through corridors overwhelmed by men whose insignia all blurred to the same colours in the darkness. "They're gone. The scavengers are coming in. Come on."

"Where—"

"Anywhere," Huyen said. She moved her hand; his came, listless, as if she'd pulled at a piece of wet cloth. "Come on."

It was only when he took a slow, faltering step—and all but collapsed on her—that she realised he'd been wounded. She bit back a curse. "Come on," she said.

"Can't." Mandias pulled away from her, shaking. "You don't have to help, you know." He took a deep, trembling breath; held it until she thought she could see light, trapped between his teeth. "I'll—"

He would heal, of course, given time. His own innate magic would come back, knitting broken bones back together, closing wounds without a scar. Given time; but he didn't have that luxury.

"You have to. We're all in this together now. Can you walk?"

Mandias closed his eyes. "I'm not sure…"

"You have to." Huyen was focused now: she knew what she had to do, and nothing else mattered. "Dozens of scavengers on the grounds, and they'll smell weakness like predators."

"They'll recognise a Fallen, too." Mandias's voice was wry. "Easy pickings."

Alive, Fallen were the bulwarks of Houses; dead, their flesh and nails and bones fuelled magic, and fetched a fortune on the black market. "Not if you hide it!" Huyen snapped. "Do you want to die here?"

"I don't—" Mandias shook his head. "I—" He said, at last. "I've never known anything else."

That sobered Huyen. She had never known anything beyond the House either; but she was thirty years old. Fallen lived for centuries, millennia: how old was Mandias? Old enough to be one of her more distant ancestors; to be worshipped at an altar with incense and apples and tangerines, and the meagre fruit one could find, in the ruins of Paris.

"Life doesn't stop here," she said, slowly, carefully. She had to believe it, or she, too, would stop here, and lie waiting for the bullet or the sword blade. She looked around the kitchen. Everything had been looted; but in one of the corners of the furnaces, there was a soot-stained, half-burnt tablecloth: it must once have been very fine—she could see the embroidery beneath the grime—but now it was irretrievable. She picked it up, and draped it over Mandias's shoulders, folding it into a hood to cover his face.

"That's not much of a disguise," Mandias said, wryly.

As if there was anything more either of them could do. Huyen bit back angry words: he was scared, and arrogant, and used to having his own way, and the last thing he needed now was to hear this from her. "Keep your head down," she said.

Mandias took one, two faltering steps: the cloth moved with him. Thank God; with the wound he had little of the effortless, instinctive grace of Fallen; though of course the illusion wouldn't last long, if anyone got a good look at him. "Let's go," she said.

He had to lean on her to walk out of the kitchen; and she felt the warmth of him against her skin, the tug of the magic within him, like the remnants of a spent fire in the hearth. The only Fallen in Aiguillon's kitchens had been Lorosa, who'd kept to herself and used her magic to make sugar confections so finely detailed it seemed they'd come alive. Huyen had never touched a Fallen, but of course she'd heard enough about it; about the thrill of magic like a forbidden drug, the heat of their skin; the feeling of tightness in one's body, as if the world had suddenly grown unbearably small.

He grew heavier against her as they walked; the ruined, scorched corridors seeming to stretch endlessly around her—surely she hadn't walked this much, to get into the kitchens—surely…?

There were other scavengers creeping into the House now; keeping a wary eye on their surroundings: two boys, darting as quick and lean as bloodhounds, as if the soldiers could be back at any moment; an old woman leaning on a younger girl, imperiously pointing with her cane at scorch marks on the wall. Their gazes met Huyen's; hung on her and Mandias—for a single, heart-stopping moment, one of the two boys frowned, looking into Mandias's face below the hood, and Huyen braced herself, unsure of whether it was to flee or to defend him; and Mandias's flesh became fever-hot to the touch, the magic within him roiling like the cut-off heads of the hydra: weakened, but eager to find something, anything that they could bite and tear apart. And then the boy's gaze moved away, and he gestured to his companion to come after him.

Huyen let out a deep, burning breath. "Come on," she whispered; and Mandias followed. He'd pulled slightly away from her: he was still limping, but he seemed to be a little bit better.

In the gardens, the corpses were unrecognisable messes: fingers hacked away for rings, bloody marks on necks where necklaces had been torn away. The scavengers had come and gone, leaving only the indignity of defiled flesh; and the way lay clear to the soot-stained streets. Huyen walked, keeping her focus on the grass—centimetre after agonising centimetre, feeling eyes on her back from within the House. Any moment now, someone was going to realise that Mandias moved wrong; that here was a wounded Fallen with no means to defend himself, and magic there for the taking…

They reached the street, and stopped. Through the haze moved soldiers—Huyen's heart missed a beat, but it looked as though they were simply regrouping, rather than paying attention to yet another pair of scavengers coming out of the House. "Let's go," she said; and became aware, after a few paces around a corner, that Mandias had stopped.

"Where?" he asked.

Huyen shrugged. "Anywhere." The ruins of the House would be swarming by nightfall: scavengers, looking for anything that hadn't been looted twice over. "Some of the other girls went to Quai Malaquais." Close to the Seine and whatever dangerous spells lurked there; but then again, whatever safe places existed were already taken over by the Houses.

Mandias shook his head. "I can't."

"Don't—" be an idiot, Huyen wanted to say, and then she realised that she was the one being an idiot. Outside the Houses, Fallen were a commodity: hated or exploited or killed for their magic. The company of their own kind was the only protection that held.

"What is it that they say? 'Fallen beyond a House's walls, stripped bones when night's blade falls.' I have to go."

"I—" She'd counted on his company without realising it. Pathetic, wasn't it—not a night without a House, and she was already yearning for the presence of a Fallen?

Mandias smiled; and it seemed to fill his entire face. "I'll come back, I promise. I owe you a debt, Huyen, and I won't forget it." And, before she could pull away, bent towards her and kissed her on the forehead—the warmth of his kiss spreading from the point of contact to her face and her body—tightening the air in her lungs until it seemed she could hardly breathe; until it felt to her that she only had to wave a hand to make sparks fly up into the air.

She'd heard the stories, of course; about Fallen; about how they could pass on magic through a kiss or a breath—but she hadn't thought—she hadn't—

She moved away, shaking. Mandias was looking at her with that odd, half-amused smile, like a man watching a filly take her first, faltering steps. "A little gift," he said. "Don't spend it rashly. I'll be back."

And, before she could work up the courage to force words through the raging storm of magic in her throat, he was gone, swallowed up by the haze of ashes as though he had never been.

Huyen stood on the edge of the steps to Quai Malaquais, and took a deep breath, trying to steady herself. Below her, the river ran black and oily, shot through with waves too strong and too disparate to come from the wind that whistled in her ears.

"You don't have to," Clarisse said, by her side.

"Of course I do," Huyen said, more sharply than she'd intended to. "We have to eat tonight."

Clarisse's hand closed on her wrist. "Don't be a fool. You're still shaken. I've seen it."

"Doesn't matter," Huyen said. "It's just stuff that happens."

"To me, yes," Clarisse said. "You're right, it's just stuff that happened. But to you? Look me in the eye, Huyen. Tell me it doesn't matter Joséphine is dead."

Huyen breathed in again; felt Mandias's magic settle in her bones, a network of pinpricks on her entire skin. It was weaker now; almost spent. And when it did run out…

Well, she'd be like Joséphine, wouldn't she?

Below, by the river's edge, was the cartload of half-melted snow the Houses of Solferino and Samothrace had dumped over the parapet, already grey and dull from the ash that was always in the air. There would be things in there—lost coins and horseshoe nails, small lost hairpins or jewellery: treasures they could barter against a ladleful of soup or a hunk of stale bread; for a minute of warmth at a fire. Treasures, if one had the guts to seize them from the river's grasp.

For the river killed.

"I can do it," Clarisse said. She'd plaited her long, lank hair; it hung down the side of her neck, smelling faintly of ashes. "Look, Huyen, it's not a House here. We don't give orders that you have to follow under pain of punishment or death."

No, not a House anymore. Just…

"I can do it," Clarisse said, again. "For both of us, if need be. Stay here."

"I—" Huyen closed her eyes, and saw again Joséphine—just by her side, working together with her, always casting a wary glance at the river. She heard, again, the rumble behind them—felt the magic rise within her, even as her leg muscles bunched up to run—to reach the safety of the stairs before it was too late—and then the scream, and Joséphine slipping over the wet cobbles, flung backwards as though seized by invisible hands—she'd looked into her friend's eyes then; and seen only the river—shades of water tinged with oil and mother-of-pearl, rising to drown everything.

I can do it, she wanted to say; but the words turned to pebbles in her mouth; dragging her down as surely as Joséphine.

"You can't," Clarisse said. She pushed Huyen slowly, gently backwards, until the parapet came up against Huyen's calves. "Wait here. I'll be back."

And then she ran down the stairs, joining the others foraging in the melting snow—dancing, nimbly, to avoid the acid spray of river water; her hands coming down with big chunks of snow, which she dusted off and threw behind her as though it was all a game.

A game that had killed Joséphine.

Huyen had crept back, that night; run to the river with magic sharpening her eyesight, slipping on wet cobbles and wondering if every misstep would be her last. And, shaking, shivering, she'd thrown three incense sticks into the waters; because one didn't know, one never knew if the spirits were watching. Nothing happened, of course. She didn't know what she'd expected—a golden turtle, rising up from the waves; or perhaps the sleek, serpentine shapes of dragons, their scales the colour of the oil spreads. Something; anything; but of course there wasn't anything like that. Of course the stories of her childhood were just myths to keep children entertained; of course rivers didn't grant blessings or good fortune, or even the two-edged sword of their attention.

Of course.

There wasn't much left in Paris; and still the Houses fought each other, like cocks locked in mortal combat. Draken and Aiguillon had fallen; and so had Hell's Toll, in the south. Huyen stared at the river, letting the magic rise within her; a warmth that reminded her of the fire in the great hall; of the furnaces that were never stopped, day or night; and the touch of Mandias's lips on her forehead…

I'll be back. I promise.

Clarisse and Manon would laugh, if she told them. An alchemist's apprentice, beholden to a former kitchen girl? And how would he find her in the teeming horde of refugees, anyway? The entire city heaved over with hunger and poverty, and he would care enough to track down one girl? No, he'd be ensconced safely in one House or another, thanking God or whatever it was that Fallen believed in for his good fortune; and he would not look back.

But still. Still, he had promised…

The noise lulled her to sleep; the distant sound of guns and explosions; the gentle patter of soot onto her clothes; the pull and tug of magic in her bones.

She woke with a start. Overhead, it was getting dark. Clarisse and the others had moved further along the quay, to another cartload of snow; nimbly dancing over the cobblestones. The air was tight, humid and heavy as if a storm hung over them; her chest ached, as if she'd run through the city, and for a moment she wasn't quite sure where she was—everything infinitely far away, the buildings of Ile de la Cité like remote mountains.

There was someone, a little further on the parapet; a mass of shadow in the growing darkness. "Mandias?" Huyen asked, but when she got closer she saw that it was a woman. "I'm sorry," she said.

The woman looked up. She was Annamite, dressed in old fashioned clothes with knot buttons; what looked like rough silk, a muddy white that seemed to glow in the diffuse light from the sky—the sun was setting, giving a faint reddish glow to everything. "It doesn't matter," the woman said. Her voice was low, cultured, with the easy accents of power.

House. Had to be. She'd never heard of any Annamite rising high in the hierarchy of Houses, but what else would the woman be? Either way, she was bad news. Huyen was Houseless now, and couldn't afford to be sucked back into the struggles of the powerful. "I'll go—"

A hand as cold as the river water closed on her fist. "Stay, please. It's not often that I see a compatriot here."

"I—" The woman's eyes seemed to glow; it wasn't sunlight, and it didn't feel like the fiery magic she'd seen in Mandias's eyes—and in any case, there weren't Annamite Fallen, the idea was just ridiculous. And then Huyen realised that the glimmer in the woman's eyes were tears. "I'm sorry," she said again; and, from the depths of memory, dredged up the tales Mother had told her in the kitchens, before the rot gnawed at her innards.

White is for mourning; rough silk or hemp—one year for wives, three years for mother or father…

"You've lost someone," Huyen said. "I'm sorry."

"Don't be." The woman's grip on her eased; but Huyen didn't move.

"Who?" she asked.

The woman shrugged, too quickly, too casually. Clarisse would have said, "Liar"; but Huyen wasn't Clarisse. She didn't have decades of eking out a living on the streets. "My father," she said. Her gaze moved; settled on the blackened river; on the patches of oily foam on the waves; the crawling, oozing shapes that seemed to move just under the surface of the war. "It wasn't quick, or pretty."

"Is it ever?" The words were out of Huyen's mouth before she could stop them. She started to mouth an apology, but the woman's raised hand stopped her. "I lost…someone, too." And so many other people; and a House; and an entire way of life; but the only memory that would come was Joséphine, slipping on the cobbles—the House had become a distant dream, one she could barely believe she'd lived through.

The woman looked at her for a while, and said nothing. "He was sick for a long time," she said, at last. "It was not…unexpected. Though…" She stared at the river for a while. "He did not expect me to ever rise to take his place."

House. She had to be House. A head of House? But none of them were Annamite, not even Shellac in the Southeast—surely she'd know, if one of them—?

But she'd never paid attention to politics, had she? Not even when she'd been in the kitchens. They were the games of the powerful, and they always harmed those at the bottom of the heap.

"I'm sure you'll do fine," Huyen said, lamely. What would a head of House be doing at this late hour of the night, in the middle of nowhere? It made no sense.

"That's...kind of you," the woman said; and looked up again, and there was a harshness in the lines of her face that hadn't been there before. "Tell me about your friend."

Green eyes, turning to the flat, muddy brown of river silt; becoming slowly transparent, as if the whites were filling with a line of water; a stifled scream in Joséphine's mouth, turning to a wet gurgle... "We were in the House together," Huyen said, slowly. "Aiguillon. Kitchen girls. Chopping greens and boning fowl, and then turning scraps into feasts, after the war started." She closed her eyes, trying to un-see Joséphine's gaze; but she couldn't. "The river took her."

Overhead, the sky was dark: night was falling. Huyen didn't move. She felt...at ease with the woman, in an odd, unspoken way—perhaps because the woman was Annamite, too, even though the last time Huyen had heard Viet spoken was when Mother had died, years and years ago—or perhaps simply because the woman understood what it meant to grieve: what Clarisse, hard-headed and practical and used to losing people, could never understand no matter how hard she tried to.

"The river always takes things," the woman said. Her voice was slow, gentle. "It used to be...different, before. Running through meadows and gardens, with children playing in the shallows."

Huyen snorted. "Did it ever?" she asked. "Centuries ago." Even in the kindest, happiest memories of her childhood, there were few gardens; except the famed ones at Hawthorn, in the southwest. Paris was a city of teeming thousands of inhabitants, not a charming countryside village.

"A long time ago," the woman said. Her hands moved, as if weaving a pattern in a secret language. "But it's changed, with the war. All those spells in the air…" She opened her hands, releasing her pattern to the sooty winds.

Huyen shivered. "The war changed everything." She'd lost the House; lost Mandias; lost Joséphine.

"It always does." The woman shook her head. "Ashes and dust and soot. Fallen magic isn't kind. It twists everything out of shape, like a cancer." She looked straight at Huyen then; and her eyes blazed with a translucent, faintly green light; like the jade bracelets Mother had treasured for so long, and then been buried with. "I shall give you advice, child, though you didn't ask for it. What you have within you—"

"How—" Huyen licked her lips; changed her mind. "I don't have anything special."

"Don't lie." The woman's voice was sharp. "It's obvious to anyone with a little bit of power. Fallen magic is a cancer, child. Don't hold on to it."

Heat rose to Huyen's cheeks coloured. "It was a gift. From a friend." But friends didn't leave, did they? Friends didn't break promises or betray…

"Whoever they are," the woman said, rising from the parapet, "they're not your friend."

"He's coming back," Huyen said; because she had to say it aloud; had to make it real. Had to believe it. "He said he would come back."

The woman's face did not move. "They never do." She paused, to pick up something from the parapet: a speck of dirt; a patch of soot? "But think on it, child." Her hand moved; encompassed the blackened river; the dark, roiling skies above; the girls down on the quay, grimy and in rags, scavenging for a bit of warmth, a bit of food. "Fallen magic is destroying us. All of us in this city, from the heads of Houses to the children cast adrift. The Houses tear each other apart, but we're the ones who will have to live on in the wreck of the city."

The fighting had moved away from the Latin Quarter after the fall of Aiguillon; for now, it could only be heard in the distant sound of explosions; in the occasional passage of bloodied soldiers through the camp where they all lived, little more than tarp stretched over half-destroyed walls. "They will have to live here too," Huyen said.

"Of course." The woman's voice was mocking. "But, however things end, they'll be on top of things, lording over us all. Isn't that always the case?"

"Who are you?" Huyen asked. "You say magic is bad, that it will destroy us. But there is nothing else, is there? It's not good intentions that will get me money, or change what's happening." She'd got used to her life, she had—everything about the House receding into the background, the hushed chatter of the kitchens at night pushed back into the farthest corners of her dreams; the elaborate meals fading until a chunk of stale bread seemed a gift from heaven. But to be so casually reminded of it; of everything she'd lost, by this woman who moved effortlessly among the powerful... "You mock the Houses, but you're the same as them, aren't you? You're rich and powerful, and you don't much care about the war."

The woman did not move. It seemed as though she was going to say something; but then her gaze fixed on Huyen's, and she shook her head. "No," she said at last. "I do care, but you're right about one thing, child. There's not much that I can offer you. I thought—" Without warning, she laid a hand on Huyen's wrist, just over the bones. Something pulsed, deep within her, not the raging fire of Fallen magic, but an older, colder thing. "Never mind. Have a good day, child. And, should you ever have need… My name is Ngoc Bich."

Ngoc Bich. Jade. A pretty, old-fashioned name for a woman. Almost too old-fashioned; a name for two generations before Huyen, the first Annamites to be brought over to the Metropole, or even older than that.

Jade, like the light in her eyes; like the cold of her skin. Mother had said something about beauty cold enough to shatter jade: it fitted Ngoc Bich well. All too well.

Ngoc Bich walked away along the length of the parapet: Huyen, rising, saw her go to the next set of stairs leading down; and calmly descend them. She waited, but Ngoc Bich never came up.

Power. Magic, and effortless wealth. Except she'd spoken of the Houses as if she were a stranger to them. Some other player in the game, then; a gang powerful enough to rival the Houses themselves? Not likely: gangs were semi-organised, but all the magical talents in the city flocked to the Houses.

Now, of course, most magical talents were dead; or busy killing each other in senseless battles. And to meddle in their affairs would see her killed, too.

Huyen's wrist ached where Ngoc Bich had touched her, as if every bone in her arm had frozen over. But it didn't matter. It would fade, in time.

She walked back to the stairs, slowly. Clarisse and the others were gone back to the camp: she would find them clustered around a fire, toasting their latest finds with alcohol acrid enough to choke. Something exploded overhead—somewhere over the Seine, in the direction of House Silverspires—and there was the distant sound of soldiers calling to one another, rallying for an assault; for something that would take down a House, just as they had taken Aiguillon down…

Huyen called up Mandias's magic, just a fraction of it; just enough to dispel the cold in her wrist; to remind her of his face when he'd kissed her and the warmth that had suffused her entire body.

They never do come back.

Should you ever have need…

It didn't matter. Or rather, she couldn't allow it to matter. Keep her head down; find worthless treasures in the snow—enough to eke out a living, day after day; to hang on until the war ended—until they stood in the ruins, and they were still at the bottom of the heap, poor and disregarded—and the future was as bleak and as devastated as the soot-encrusted streets.

No. It wouldn't be like that. Not for her. Mandias would come back. He would rescue her, as he had promised; bring her back to a House, where she'd find her place again, where she could belong; where she could be safe.

She had to hold on to that thought; but in her mind all she could feel was the cold touch of Ngoc Bich's hand on her wrist, and the feeling that the river, rising, would drown her as it had drowned Joséphine.

❦

For Christmas, everyone in the camp put together their meagre savings, and bartered for fresh bread, firewood and a chunk of meat from the black market. It was tough, rangy flesh from an animal that must have been used as a beast of burden before it was butchered, but Clarisse threw herself into preparations with the enthusiasm of a child.

Huyen put together a few faded spices, and set the pot with the meat to braise on glowing embers: warmth and fire all day, a luxury she'd almost forgotten. "I'm not sure about the taste," she said, sprinkling a little salt into the pot. Eugenie and Theophraste had picked up some of the younger ones, and had gone to have a fight in the muddy snow. Huyen felt…old. Used up. If she called up Mandias's magic, there was only silence within her; and a flicker of warmth like the last breath of a dying man. It was gone; or close enough; and he wouldn't be coming back for her.

"You worry too much," Clarisse said. "It's going to be great."

"And a welcome change, too," Manon said. She was one of the kitchen girls who'd come over: her and Eugenie and Joséphine. She seldom spoke; and was busy nursing her two-month-old son, bundled up in all the blankets Clarisse and Huyen could gather. "Christmas should be different."

It did feel different: the air tight and cold with a bite of ice; and only a distant rumble from other parts of the city. Except it changed nothing, did it? "Christmas truce," Clarisse said, with a bitter laughter.

"Some of them do believe in God," Huyen said, slowly. "Not all Fallen..."

"And not all Houses?" Clarisse laughed. She finished wrapping a garland—little more than scraps of coloured cloths sewn together—around one of the ruined walls. "If you wish. It's Christmas, after all. We should be charitable." She grew serious again. "How are you?"

"I'm fine." Huyen coloured. "Really."

"Don't think so," Manon said. "You've hardly spoken, these past few days." The baby whimpered; she shifted positions to offer him the other breast.

"I don't have to speak." Huyen stirred the pot, and put the cracked lid over it. "I'm fine. Really." But she wasn't. She would wake up in the middle of the night with a gasp, wondering what the point of it was—what purpose there was, in living day after day with no prospect of a better future. Everything seemed... grimmer than it should have been. "Really," she said.

Clarisse shook her head. "I think you shouldn't go down tomorrow. It's Christmas Day anyway—not going to be a lot of people."

"There'll be pickings, though," Huyen said. Everyone would have put on their best clothes, and gone from House to House to celebrate: they would have lost elegant scarves and hats, pendants of pearls or gems—things worth a fortune—and of course the camp would need her to pull her weight.

"Don't worry about pickings," Clarisse said. "Just get some rest."

"I'm no beggar." And no cripple.

"Of course you're not," Manon said, soothingly. "But—" She shook her head, slowly. "Look, Clarisse is right. You went down for her when she had that cough, didn't you? Same thing."

Huyen wasn't weak. She wasn't in need of help—or, rather, the one she needed help from wasn't around. It was too much to hope he would find her; that he'd somehow walk through the city's blanket of snow on Christmas Day and find her, shivering around the fire…

Clarisse looked back at her garlanded wall, critically. "Hmm. It will have to do. Now come help me with the plates."

They hunkered in the shadow of the wall, eating the meat-rich soup: an extravagance that was almost sickening. "Well," Clarisse said. "That was good. Thanks, Huyen."

Huyen shrugged. "I can at least do this. It's not much compared to a House kitchen." It had tasted of nothing—of ashes and grit, like every meal had for a while—ever since the magic had started to die down within her. Why couldn't she forget that she was losing it?

"Of course not." Clarisse grinned. "But worth as much as their foie gras and their venison and their chestnuts."

Huyen forced a smile. There had only been meat in Aiguillon's kitchens: the war had cut off supplies from the suburbs. The foie gras and the venison only existed in Clarisse's dreams; but it didn't seem to matter either way. "It's not bad, I'll grant you."

Manon set down her plate; and re-adjusted her grip on the baby. She glanced at Clarisse, who nodded, looking uncannily serious.

"What is it?" Huyen asked.

Manon reached out behind her, in the shadow of the wall, and withdrew a long, wrapped package.

"I know we don't do gifts," Clarisse said, "but we thought—" her voice trailed away. "Oh, Hell. Just open it, will you?" Her face was set, in that familiar expression: she didn't like what she was doing, but she thought it was the right thing, all the same.

Inside, there was a crude wooden box, which was warm to the touch. Someone had attempted to carve letters into it, but had given up halfway through, leaving only gouges in the wood. It was warm; warmer than it should have been, after being left in the cold for hours. Huyen removed the lid; and the familiar feeling hit her, then.

Angel essence.

It smelled…old, musty, like rotten books, but it didn't matter, because all she could feel was the fire—all she could think of was what it would feel like to inhale the essence; to have again that sweet, sweet rush of power in her bones, that reminder of Mandias…. Her hands were shaking; she stilled them, with an effort.

Clarisse's face was set. "We couldn't afford much. Essence is bloody expensive, and that's going to be the last you see until next year."

"At best," Manon said. The baby was asleep against her chest, wrapped in a woollen scarf; his face slack and peaceful, utterly contented.

"I—" Huyen tried to say something; felt only the sharp, acrid taste of magic on her tongue. "I—"

"Just be careful." Clarisse frowned. "That stuff's bad for your lungs."

She didn't need to say it was addictive; of course Huyen already knew that. It had been illegal in Aiguillon; not because it was ground Fallen bones decanted into a drug, but because it was addictive; and because it killed.

But then, so many things did, those days.

"Thank you," Huyen said; and hugged them, one after the other—hard, as if she could make up for her unpleasantness earlier on.

"Be careful," Clarisse said. They watched her, both of them—their faces frozen in an emotion Huyen couldn't quite read—fear or love; or anger, rigidly controlled? And, in the distant light of the fire, they suddenly felt like strangers to her; like masks over stringless puppets, insinuated into her new, meaningless life—suddenly the circle around the wall was too small, too stifling, and she ran away into the night, clutching the warmth of the Fallen magic to her chest.

She found herself by the river; because everything in Paris always came back to the river—because, even blackened, even polluted, it was still life and death and everything in between; because it was the river's arms that would carry her and drown her, when her time came—like Joséphine's time had come.

She sat on the parapet with the box in her hands. It was warm: fire, rekindled, a conflagration that would engulf her, if she gave it a chance.

Be careful, Clarisse whispered in her mind, and Huyen had no answer for her. It was magic: not Mandias's magic, with so little of the kiss she remembered; so little of the hope she'd carried with her, all that time. But still…

Still, it was warmth in her bones; and sunlight casting everything in a different hue: the world shifting and turning until it was once more a place she could live in; somewhere she dared to feel joy; to feel hope. All that, and more.

"You didn't heed my advice, I see."

Ngoc Bich.

Huyen scrambled to stand up, trying to hide the wooden box from view. Why was she feeling like a child caught out with a forbidden treat? "It was a gift," she said, colour rising to her cheeks.

"Indeed." Ngoc Bich coalesced out of the darkness, as if she had always been there. She wore a dress as red as blood, with ample sleeves trailing in the wind; the embroidery dragons on it faded, half-unravelled, so that in the dim light they seemed to be faceless monsters with half a snout, and eyes reduced to thin pinpoints of whiteness. "It's a time for gifts, isn't it." It wasn't a question.

She walked slowly, steadily towards Huyen; her eyes the colour of jade, and the shadow of something behind her—not wings like a Fallen, but a hint of something else, something that tied her to her power—her gaze hard, pitiless. She would crush Huyen without a second thought, if she thought her a danger.

"Who—" Huyen struggled to get words through her dry throat. "Who are you? What do you want?"

Ngoc Bich stopped, head cocked. "Think of me…as a friend."

"You're—" You're not my friend, Huyen wanted to say, but that would have been suicide. At least the others were back in the camp, safely ensconced by the fire. At least it was just her.

What was she? Not a Fallen. Not a magician. Someone…

She didn't want to voice her suspicions aloud. She didn't dare.

Ngoc Bich came closer. Huyen braced herself for the burst of magic; but, instead, Ngoc Bich reached out, and gently closed the box of essence. "I don't have much company," Ngoc Bich said, gently. "Or many countrymen."

"I'm not from Annam." She was French. She'd been born in Paris; she would die in Paris. That she happened to look different, and remember snatches of another language—should have been irrelevant.

But of course it was not. Of course Ngoc Bich reminded her of other times; of Mother in the kitchen, whispering the old tales and myths to her. "We're from different worlds," she said, slowly.

"Perhaps." Ngoc Bich was close; close enough that she could feel the cold, rising to engulf her. "But we won't ever get closer to each other with that logic, will we?"

"Do I want to get closer?" Bold and brash, and utterly inappropriate. She could have kicked herself.

Ngoc Bich drew back, as if she'd been physically hurt. She didn't say anything for a while. "You were kind, child. It's a rare thing, these days. Rare enough for me to notice." She put her hand on the parapet; as if to steady herself. "As I said, it's a time for gifts. And for miracles, sometimes." She withdrew her hand, leaving something Huyen couldn't quite see. But then she did, and it was as though someone were twisting a fist of ice around her belly.

Three sodden incense-sticks, still bearing the marks where she'd struggled to light them.

"You're—" she whispered. "You're—" She couldn't say the word aloud after all, but it came up in her mind, all the same. *Rong.*

Dragon. The spirits of water, the spirits of rain; living in their kingdoms beneath the waves: those who sent the rain and the good harvests; and the storms that swept up the unwary and destroyed livelihoods. "You're the river. You—"

Joséphine's eyes, filling with water, and the colour of mud and silt—her hand, gradually torn away from Huyen—all the magic in Huyen rising, trying to save Joséphine, knowing it would be too late, that it had been too late from the moment she'd been seized by the river…

"Close enough," Ngoc Bich said.

"You—" You killed Joséphine. You're killing us, one by one. "You don't grant gifts, or wishes. You just kill."

"As I said—" Ngoc Bich's face was bitter—"many things changed, with the war."

"That's not an excuse!"

"No, of course not." Ngoc Bich withdrew, slowly, carefully. She pointed to the three incense sticks on the parapet. "I can't do much. But I came to remind you of this—that all prayers are answered, eventually, if you wish hard enough."

And then she was gone, and Huyen was left alone on the parapet, cradling the box of angel essence—utterly unsure of what to think or pray for.

On Christmas Day, the city was silent. Huyen woke up at dawn, and wandered the camp; finding only Manon up with her child, and Theophraste, indefatigable, folding up garlands. The remains of last night's dinner were warming up on the embers; Huyen gave them a stir, and settled down with her box in a quiet corner, away from where anyone could see her.

Her sleep had been dark, and disturbed. She'd seen Ngoc Bich, her hair uncoiling and twisting itself into the antlers of a deer; her skin slowly turning into opalescent scales, the shape of a twisted pearl appearing below her lips—beautiful and awe-inspiring and so terribly corrupted. She'd gestured; and the stairs leading to the quay, wreathed in mist, became the entrance to a pagoda, except that the red paint was peeling, and the longevity tiles were cracked; and the smell of rot wafted from it, the churning mud of the river; the water, rising to cover everything…

A sound made her look up—at first distant, then gaining in intensity, a dull, distant roar like gunfire that finally resolved into the roar of a motor.

Here?

The car was sleek and black, moving with the smoothness of predators on the prowl. It nosed into the camp as if its place had already been there; braked and parked, scattering the embers from the fire all over the plaza. It shimmered with magic; with the heat that had replaced the gas in the tank; with the mass of shimmering wards that protected its occupants from any stray spells or explosions.

House.

It was bad news. Could not be anything else.

Theophraste moved towards where the others slept—running, his face reshaping itself around rising panic; Manon slid away, hiding herself behind a wall. Huyen got up, one hand diving into the wooden box, scattering angel essence over herself—feeling the fire on her skin, the promise of power—the promise of safety, no matter the price. She only had to inhale; but her hand clenched around the essence, and would not rise higher. The price was too high. She could not pay it. She could not…

The car's door opened. First came a handful of bodyguards, carrying rifles, deploying around the plaza—speaking to each other with jabs and hand-gestures, spreading in dreadful silence—Huyen had forgotten, how threatening it could all be; how effortlessly they seemed to own a place.

Then came an older woman—a personal maid, with a supercilious frown on her face—and, after her, the last two people in the car.

They were both wearing black and silver—Hawthorn, then, the House that controlled the southwest of Paris—and both wore elegant, old-fashioned suits, with swallow-tail jackets and top hats. They were both Fallen: the older one wore rectangular, horn-rimmed glasses; and the other, the younger…

Mandias.

Huyen's breath caught in her throat. It was him, but he had changed, and not changed: the same lean, earnest face; but the limp and the scars were gone, and he held himself with the easy arrogance of the powerful. His gaze moved around the camp, sweeping everything as though assessing its worth; and stopped, unerringly, on Huyen.

He didn't say anything. He didn't need to. Huyen, frozen like a deer in the headlights, watched him, his companion and the maid walk closer—slowly, agonisingly slowly, sauntering with sickening casualness.

Closer, and closer; and then Mandias was enfolding her in his embrace. She felt the heat of his magic roil over her, filling her to bursting—it should have made her whole, should have given the world its edge back, but it didn't—she felt as though she was going to retch.

"Mandias. I wasn't expecting you," she whispered, because she didn't know what else to say.

Mandias laughed; quick, easy; hurtful. "This is Huyen," he said to his companion. "She saved my life."

The companion watched her, for a while. He had eyes that seemed to change colour as the light shifted, from grey to green. His gaze was lightly amused. "I see," he said. "The kitchen girl."

It should have been mocking, but it wasn't.

"I waited for you," Huyen said to Mandias. She was…utterly bereft of words, feeling nothing but the roiling of Mandias's magic, a storm that seemed to twist her stomach into knots. "I thought—"

"I'm sorry," Mandias said. "It took me longer than I thought to find you. I shouldn't have left you." He moved a hand, encompassed the entire camp. "I know it's been bad for you here, for far too long."

It hadn't been bad; not all of it—there was Clarisse, and Manon, and…But the words wouldn't leave Huyen's throat.

"But it doesn't matter. I asked Asmodeus and Lord Uphir, and there's no need for this anymore. You can come with us."

"With you?" Huyen asked, slowly, stupidly.

"Back to Hawthorn!" Mandias's smile slipped, slightly. "Back under the protection of a House. That's where you've always belonged. Come," he said, extending a hand to her.

It was what she'd always wanted; what she'd dreamt of, the thought that had kept her going day and night; that Mandias would come back, that he would find her, pay his debt to her. That she'd go back, one way or another. That she would…

The other Fallen—Asmodeus, had to be—watched her. She couldn't read the expression in his eyes. "I have seen more enthusiasm. People would kill, for this. Especially now."

"Come," Mandias said. "This—eyesore—isn't the place for you."

Huyen turned, to look at the camp. Manon was gone; she caught a glimpse of Theophraste, crouching behind one of the ruined walls, watching her warily: of course, the two Fallen could level the camp if they felt like it. An eyesore, Mandias had said.

Asmodeus watched her, slowly, carefully; watched her slowly walk towards Mandias. Waiting to see her reaction, Huyen knew, with agonising clarity. He was amused by her, as one might be by an insect which had started to talk.

"You could be so many things in Hawthorn," Mandias was saying. "There's space in the kitchens, of course, but the laboratories also need hands, and if you wanted you could go back to the school, and be so much more than a servant—"

Servants. Like the conscripted soldiers watching the camp with hardened eyes, so still they barely seemed human anymore; or the personal maid, now walking by her side with obvious disapproval on her face.

Asmodeus's eyes held her; mocked her—the colour of ashes, of gardens gone to cinders. Huyen forced words out of her mouth, feeling the taste of grit on her tongue. "Houses don't take people like me."

"Of course not," the maid snorted. "Consider yourself fortunate—you're nothing but the riffraff of the streets."

Asmodeus held up a hand; and the maid fell silent instantly, with an expression Huyen knew all too well. Fear. "You will not speak out of turn," he said. And then, to Huyen, with the same tone, velvet wrapped around an iron blade, "Consider it…a favour to Mandias. His little pet, brought back into the fold."

Mandias was still talking, about all the things she could do, once in Hawthorn; of all the decisions he'd make for her. A pet. That was what she would be, in the House. Clarisse would have laughed. She'd have said it was worth it, wasn't it, to be fed and clothed and protected. But Clarisse was behind the walls with the others, waiting for the House to leave—praying that they wouldn't decide to cleanse the camp; just because they felt like it.

She'd be like the soldiers; like the maid—bought and owned and kept in fear and mindless obedience. What was it that Ngoc Bich had said: that Fallen magic twisted everything out of shape?

"I—" Huyen took in a deep, shaking breath. "I can't do it."

Mandias stopped; turned. "You can't be serious," he said. "What are you going to do?"

"I—" Huyen shook her head. "I don't know."

"Do you know how much I had to do, to get you in? How many favours I had to pull in? Do you—" His hand moved, grabbed her wrist; pulled—towards the yawning maw of the car opening, a dark opening against the ruined buildings. "You're coming with us."

No.

Her other hand was free, and still holding the box—she dipped into it, brought the angel essence to her nose—inhaled, felt the power rise in her like liquid fire, a constriction in her lungs that tore her body apart. "No," she said; and, pushing back Mandias's hand, ran for the river.

She was blind, and the magic coursed within her; nothing like the faint memory of what Mandias had left her, but raw power, primal and unfettered, every part of her burning up like kindling in a hearth—her heart like a gong within her, every beat tearing her ribs apart; her entire body feeling too tight and too small for her.

And then it was gone, and she was left on the edge of the stairs, panting—the gray of the sky too painfully bright, the river below roaring like a torrent in the spring; and little spots like dying stars dotted across her field of vision.

Through the haze, she saw them, walking towards her. Slowly, calmly, as if there were no hurry; Mandias's face twisted in anger, his hands wreathed in the light of magic; Asmodeus more leisurely, still bearing that distant expression of amusement.

There was nothing but the river at her back, now; and no way forward but the House.

"Who do you think you are," Mandias said. His face was awful to behold; the angel before the Fall; the shadow of wings at his back, black and flame-infused. "You little good-for-nothing. Do you think you can just say no to us, like that?"

That was no way forward.

Huyen turned, and ran downstairs, to the river.

She stood, shaking, on the quay, in the churned mud over the cobblestones—they came on, of course they did, walking downstairs with barely a pause; although Asmodeus now had wards pulled around him; and was going far more slowly than his companion. Mandias, of course, was past caring. He would find her and drag her to the House; and hold her there if he had to. He would…

She still had the box in her hand; the angel essence—magic, but it would be of no use to her. Not against two experienced Fallen. Raw power wouldn't avail her anything.

All prayers are answered, if you wish hard enough.

If you—

"Ngoc Bich," she whispered, as Mandias cleared the bottom of the steps. "Please."

For a moment—a terrible, suspended moment—she thought nothing would happen; that she had misheard or misunderstood what Ngoc Bich had told her. She backed towards the wall of the embankment—a wall at her back, a place where she knew she could make her last, useless stand…

But then there was a distant noise; she'd expected the roar of waves, but instead it was the slow, insistent banging of a gong; and the noise of a bell. Gradually, the river grew still, everything taking on the sickly sheen of oil or soap; and the shadow of a bridge arched over the dark waters; a covered structure with sloped roofs and a wooden railing, broken into several places.

Across the bridge walked Ngoc Bich.

She looked like the stuff of Huyen's nightmares: still wearing the old-fashioned dress with the worn embroidered dragons, but her face was no longer human: the skin flaked in patches, showing dull scales; and broken-off antlers sprouted from her head—her ample robes trailed behind her, coiling and uncoiling like the body of a snake. Her eyes were the colour of jade struck by sunlight; and the pearl below her mouth was cleaved in two, its lustre since long lost.

When she stepped onto the stones of the quay, the river came with her, clinging to her like the dress of a bride. "Well," she said. "What do we have here." It was not a question.

Huyen struggled to find her voice; but Mandias had no such qualms.

"She's mine," he said.

Ngoc Bich's gaze moved from him to Huyen; transfixed Huyen like a spear. She was…utterly inhuman, not a fellow compatriot, but the river that took and took and killed. "Is she now."

"Have you a prior claim?" Mandias asked. Light streaked from him—tendrils dipping towards the river, withdrawing as if stung.

Huyen found her voice at last, dragging it from wherever it had fled. "No," she said. "I'm not his. I don't want to go with him. I never will."

Asmodeus had stopped, halfway down the stairs; now he walked faster, and laid a hand on Mandias's shoulder. "Don't be a fool," he said. And, bowing, low, to Ngoc Bich. "Lady. We will not interfere."

"You—" Mandias turned back to Asmodeus, his face suffused with anger. "You would let this pass? It's an insult to the House!"

Asmodeus smiled. He had not moved; but he seemed to tower over Mandias; the shadow of wings at his back as sharp and as cutting as razor-blades. "The House has better things to do than worry about your pet projects, Mandias. And better uses for its time than a war with the Seine."

Ngoc Bich smiled. "You'd do well to remember this. You aren't welcome here."

"Of course," Asmodeus said. "I will remind Lord Uphir of this; and of the old treaties." Something in the way he said this—the way his voice lingered on the syllables of Uphir's name—suggested he had no liking for Lord Uphir, none at all. He dragged Mandias back; effortlessly, as if he'd got hold of a disobedient infant. "And I will…take the appropriate measures to see that this one doesn't bother you again."

Huyen shivered. She didn't want to know what Asmodeus considered appropriate measures; but, if it meant she was safe…

And then they were both gone; and it was just her and Ngoc Bich.

Ngoc Bich still looked inhuman; though less terrible; the light around her frayed and dimmed, the clothes shrunk back to mere tattered silk; her eyes brown with the barest hint of green jade.

"Dragon Empress," Huyen whispered; remembering the old myths. "That's what you are, isn't it? The river."

"A small part of it," Ngoc Bich said, softly. "As I said—Fallen magic changed everything."

Huyen shivered. "It has. Thank you."

Ngoc Bich shrugged. "It was not much. What will you do now, child?"

"I—" Huyen stared at the steps; thought of the camp and of Manon and Clarisse and all the others. "I don't know. I—"

"—didn't think it through?" Ngoc Bich smiled, darkly amused. "Perhaps you should have gone with them."

Never. "My place is here," Huyen said.

"Qualms of conscience over friendships? War isn't a time for grand moral stands."

Huyen smiled. "As good a time as any." And, aghast at her own boldness, "In the old days, there was the blessing of the river."

"Good fortune, and abundant crops?" Ngoc Bich's smile was bitter. "As you said—the days of the Seine meandering through idyllic countryside are long gone." She made a gesture, with the ample sleeves of her dress. "I can give you luck, and my protection. You won't starve, or die of cold. But it won't be much of a life: the occasional fortunate find; the occasional helpful meeting. Enough to stretch to your friends, quite probably, but not much more. It won't be much of anything."

But more than what she had, all the same. "Nevertheless…I'll take it."

"Then have my blessing." Ngoc Bich raised a hand, and laid it on Huyen's head; and the same feeling of coldness spread to her hair and the skin of her forehead; the touch of the river; the same thing that had drowned Joséphine. Her hand, convulsing, opened; and let fall the wooden box with the angel essence; it spilled at her feet, scattering magic like embers in a snowstorm. "For what it's worth, in this day and time, child."

Ngoc Bich stepped away, bowing; walked back along the bridge, which was already vanishing. Huyen, standing on the quay, watched her until she was utterly gone; until the river ran black and angry and soot-stained once more, as if nothing had ever happened.

Then, slowly, carefully picking her way on the damp cobblestones, she walked back to the stairs; and to the camp where Clarisse and Manon would be waiting.

Have my blessing. For what it's worth, in this day and time.

It won't be much of anything.

Day after day and night after night; and enough food in her belly, and fire to keep her warm; and friends by her side—not a House, never a House; but enough to keep her going until the war ended—and perhaps even beyond it, into an age where the city would be utterly changed, and the old rules didn't apply anymore.

No, not much of anything; but more than enough.

One Hundred Ablutions

JACQUELINE CAREY

As far as Keren childhoods go, I suppose mine was happy enough. Da was a picker in an omichaya orchard, and the overseer let workers take home any fruit that was rotten-ripe or too damaged to serve to our Shaladan masters. Anyone caught damaging fruit on purpose got a whipping for it, but Da didn't get caught often. My brother and sister and I almost always had enough to eat, although sometimes we had gripy bellies and loose bowels from too much omichaya.

What we didn't eat, Ma traded in the market. You could find almost anything that grew, flew, crept, crawled or swam in the whole Kerentari valley on display in the market: Fruit, fish, fowl, frogs, rice, spices, eels, eggs, nuts, wriggly bugs and crunchy grubs. There were fineries, too—intricately patterned carpets, shiny jewelry, bowls of hammered copper or finely turned wood, leather belts and sandals, tinkling brass bells and the like, but those were reserved for the Shaladan.

It seems strange to me now, but I didn't give much thought to the Shaladan when I was a child. They were simply a fact of existence, pacing slowly through the market with their long, grave faces and their long, flowing robes, at least half again as tall as the Keren servants trotting beside them, arms laden with their masters' purchases. The Shaladan women wore headscarves in muted colors and dangling earrings. The men wore turbans and wide belts from which hung long swords.

They were the Shaladan and they ruled us. What was there to think? As a Keren peasant child, I was as far beneath their notice as a grub and they were distant from my comprehension as the clouds drifting overhead.

The handmaids of Shakrath, now that was another matter. Spirits save me, I used to *envy* them.

Mind you, that was long before I was chosen.

According to the Shaladan, they're bestowing a tremendous honor on Keren girls by choosing us to serve as handmaids of Shakrath. Yes, well, I suppose they would think so, since Shakrath is *their* god and they spend large portions of their daily life in prayer and meditation. The fact that despite several centuries of occupation, the Keren haven't embraced the worship of Shakrath is irrelevant to them.

Shakrath is great; therefore, it is a great honor to serve him.

In fairness, I'll grant that there's a certain logic to their thinking, since Shakrath in his mercy and wisdom granted his people's prayers and allowed them to conquer the valley centuries ago. Before that conquest, the Shaladan were a desert folk eking out a miserable existence in a harsh terrain.

Of course, I knew none of that as a child. As a child, I only knew that the handmaids of Shakrath, with their blue robes and shaven heads and elegant strands of silver chain hanging around their necks, were special. They were granted a status that no other Keren enjoyed. Ordinary Keren weren't permitted to address them. Ordinary Keren weren't even *allowed* to wear dyed fabrics or jewelry, not even the merchants who procured such items for their Shaladan patrons. The handmaids were sleek and glossy with health. They went about their sacred task with solemn dignity, fetching great silver bowls of water from the river so that each and every member of the Shaladan household that they served might perform the ritual One Hundred Ablutions each and every day.

I certainly had no understanding of what *that* meant.

Now, I wish I didn't.

It was rumored that the handmaids did not live in squalid, over-crowded quarters like other Keren servants, but lived almost as a full-fledged member of the household in spacious rooms with windows open to the sunlight and sweet spice-tinted breezes of the valley. It was rumored that they were privileged to dine on the leavings of the household meals, which included meats traditionally forbidden to the Keren—pork, goat and beef, meats that the Shaladan say Shakrath has decreed only for the enjoyment of his own people.

It was *known* that Keren girls chosen to serve as handmaids of Shakrath were considered inviolate. No hand might be raised against them without invoking the wrath of the Shaladan. As for those handmaids' hands...well, those hands would never be given in marriage. As far as the Shaladan were concerned, the handmaids were wedded to Shakrath and would remain virgin for the entirety of their lives. It was worth a Keren boy's life to flirt with a handmaid of Shakrath, and none in his right mind would attempt it.

At six, eight, even ten years of age, this didn't sound like such a bad bargain in exchange for the perquisites.

At fourteen, with my breasts budding and handsome boys vying for my favors, I felt otherwise. I was enjoying the first taste of the power a desirable young woman can wield over men, and I liked it. I liked it *very* much, and I wanted more of it.

But it was not to be.

As a peasant, I should not even have been eligible for the lottery, but there was a bout of flux that year that left a shortage of Keren girls from the merchant class that the Shaladan preferred. And so the Shaladan priests canvassed the hovels clustered outside the walls of the city, searching for likely candidates.

I recall the long shadow of the Shaladan priest darkening our doorway. "This one is comely," he said to Da in the slow, deliberate way of his kind, pointing a finger at me. "Bring her to the lottery."

Da bowed.

I wept.

Ma wept, slapped me for weeping, and wept some more. My little brother Joji wept, too. If my older sister Juna had not been wed that very year and gone to live with her husband and his parents, she might have wept, too.

The lottery was held in the city square on the first day of the next new moon. Thirty girls had been selected, but only ten of us would be chosen to serve as handmaids. It was a simple affair. A Shaladan priest presided over an urn filled with white and black stones. Each girl reached into the urn and drew a stone.

Black meant you were free to go. White meant Shakrath had chosen you, and that was the end of life as you'd known it.

"May Shakrath bless you," the priest intoned when it was my turn. It was the nearest I'd ever been to one of the Shaladan. At close range, I could see that his sand-colored skin was slightly pebbled. "Pray that he guides your hand."

In silent defiance, I prayed to the Keren spirits of field and stream instead, thrusting my hand into the urn and drawing out a stone.

It was white.

The priest pointed toward the group of chosen girls, waiting patiently beneath the supervision of an older handmaid whom I was told to call Mistress Elia.

Numb with shock and fury, I stumbled through the rest of the day. Mistress Elia led the novitiates to the temple where we were bathed, our heads were shaved, and we were given clean blue robes to wear. I wept to see my glossy black hair lying in a pile and was slapped for it.

"It will do you no good to whine," Mistress Elia said firmly. "You'll have an easy life. Be grateful for it."

I tried. Spirits save me, I did. We all did. There were two other girls rescued from far greater hardship than me that genuinely *were* grateful. But the rest of us…no. Our lives had been stolen from us.

We received a month's instruction at the temple on the proper etiquette for fetching water and the history of the One Hundred Ablutions. Three hundred years ago, the Shaladan were a tribe of nomads roaming a drought-stricken desert. When the well in their last oasis began to fail, Shakrath sent their chieftain a vision of a lush green valley where the Shaladan might make a new home. In accordance with this singular vision, the chieftain warned his people that it would not be won without bloodshed and made a sacred vow that if the valley became theirs, every member of the Shaladan tribe would perform a daily ritual of one hundred ablutions as a meditation on their gratitude for the life-saving water and in atonement for any innocent blood spilled in the process.

So it came to pass, and the handmaids were chosen among the Keren so that we might be given the honor of bearing witness to the Shaladan expressing gratitude and atonement for slaughtering a large number of our people.

Oh, well, thank you so very much!

The galling thing was that the Shaladan genuinely *did* expect us to be grateful. At the time of their conquest, the Kerentari valley was occupied by the Jagan, a fierce and godless mountain tribe. Overpowered by the Shaladan, the Jagan abandoned the valley and fled back to the highlands. In the Shaladan view of history, they freed the poor, hapless Keren from oppression and brought us the word of Shakrath, and we were the luckier for it on both counts.

"Do you believe it's true?" I whispered at night to Shoni, the two of us sharing a pallet. She was a merchant's daughter with whom I'd struck up a friendship. "Three hundred years later, *are* we better off under the Shaladan?"

"*We* aren't, you and I." If anything, Shoni was more disgruntled than me at being chosen. Her father had been on the verge of arranging a very good marriage for her. "At least our people could mingle with the Jagan. There are still Keren in the north who trade with them," she whispered. "My Da's heard tales. They say the Jagan have eyes like cats and can see in the dark." She put her mouth close to my ear, close enough to tickle. "And they're very, very virile!"

I giggled and someone shushed us.

"The men take pride in pleasing their women at least three times a night!" Shoni reached between my thighs and squeezed. "Think about that, Dala!"

I shoved her away. "You think about it!"

She rolled onto her back and folded her arms under her head. "Oh, I do." Her voice was grim. "Every day."

In truth, so did I. But there wasn't a blessed thing either of us could do about it.

The days slipped away like water held in cupped hands, and the month was gone before it seemed scarce begun. One by one, this year's novitiates were declared full-fledged handmaids and presented to their Shaladan households. Shoni and I wept on each other's shoulders and declared eternal friendship. Although we would see each other every day as we went to and fro fetching water for our new masters, etiquette forbade us to do more than exchange the most banal of greetings.

I was nervous and jittery when my time came, balking on the path that led to my new home. The great looming house built of blocks of yellowish stone was like the Shaladan themselves, too big and too solid to comprehend. Mistress Elia sighed and tugged me by the hand. "Come, Dala."

What choice had I?

None, then.

So.

This, then, was to be my new life. I was to serve as handmaid of Shakrath to the household of Farad Dhoul, which included his wife Alaya, his daughters Atika and Amina, and their governess Resalin. On the doorstep of the house, Mistress Elia placed the first strand of silver chain around my neck, symbolizing my formal entry into service as a handmaid. For every year that I served, I would receive one additional strand. Upon entry into the house, the elderly Keren handmaid that I was to replace presented me with the ritual silver bowl, her crabbed hands trembling with the effort. I could not imagine how she'd carried out her duties for so long. She was nearly stooped under the accumulated weight of silver necklaces that she wore.

A lifetime wasted, that's what those strands represented, but I kept that thought to myself.

A silent Keren servant led me to my new quarters, careful to avoid meeting my gaze. I trailed in his wake, balancing the empty silver bowl on my head and steadying it with both hands as etiquette dictated. The rumors regarding our lodgings were true. My room on the upper story of the house was vast and spacious, with arched windows open to the warm, spice-scented breezes.

And there, I and my bowl were left alone.

Sometime before sunset, the same servant brought me a platter of food. Table scraps, maybe—but oh, what scraps they were! I ate sparingly of the rich meat lest I make myself sick. Afterward, I slept on a pallet stuffed with soft cotton.

And yet the luxury I'd coveted as a child did nothing to allay my loneliness.

At dawn, the bell that summoned me to my duty rang, a single loud scintillating chime. I rose, descended the stair, unlocked the main door, and made the first of what would be many, many long treks to fetch water from the river.

Keep your steps graceful. Keep your bowl balanced. Keep your countenance serene. Keep your thoughts fixed on your duty.

Do not glance around you. Do not acknowledge Keren commoners. Do not dawdle or delay. Do not splash. Do not allow the hem of your robe to trail in the river. Do not make idle chatter with other handmaids.

Do not *spill.*

That last one was the one that terrified me. I'd practiced in the temple, but there was no room for mistakes now. The punishment for spilling the first time was a reprimand. Second, a day's fast. A third spill earned a visit to the temple and a whipping from Mistress Elia.

After that...well, Mistress Elia had been vague. But she was very clear on the ultimate punishment for a handmaid judged unfit to serve Shakrath: Banishment. Oh, and not just banishment from the city. No, a handmaid found unfit to serve would be taken beyond the Kerentari valley twenty leagues into the desert and abandoned to Shakrath's ungentle mercy.

Hence, my fear.

Nonetheless, I managed to fill my bowl and return without spilling a drop. All Shaladan households are laid out in the same manner and I found the sun terrace exactly where I'd been taught it would be. There was the tripod for the bowl, there was the stand with the golden bell and hammer, there was the carved wooden rest for the silver ladle, and there was the mat for me to kneel upon. I lowered the bowl carefully and placed it in the tripod. The water showed me my unfamiliar reflection in the early morning light—my head as bald as an egg, silver glinting around my throat.

I looked away from my reflection, took up the hammer and gave the golden bell a single sharp tap, then knelt on the mat.

Soon enough, Farad Dhoul came in response to the bell's summons. As head of the household, it was his privilege to perform the day's first ritual. Hearing his slow, deliberate steps, I kept my eyes downcast.

He halted in front of the bowl. All I could see of him were his immense sandal-shod feet with their splayed toes and horny yellow nails. "What is your name, handmaid?"

Having been addressed, I looked up. "Dala, master."

"Dala." He stooped to touch the top of my head. "Be welcome in the service of Shakrath."

Not trusting myself to speak, I nodded.

Apparently that sufficed, for without giving me another thought, he commenced the ritual. I watched him unwind his turban and hang it on the stand. Beneath the cloth, his head was as hairless as mine. The pebbled texture of his tannish hide was more pronounced on the dome of his skull. Kneeling in his presence, I could not help but be terribly conscious of how different the Shaladan were from us. Beneath the folds of his robe I could discern the faint outline of his long backward-bending legs with hocks instead of knees, built for striding great distances across the desert sands on those wide, splayed horn-nailed feet. A nictitating membrane protected his eyes and the narrow nostrils of his long nose could pinch almost completely closed—against sand-storms, one supposes. A not-entirely-unpleasant scent of hot dust emanated from his skin.

A tall man for his kind, he was nearly twice my height. I felt small and weak by comparison. My soft Keren skin, as dark and rich a brown as the kui-nuts that grew in the valley's shady groves, offered little protection from harsh elements, little more than the sweeping lashes of my eyes. The thin, pale nails of my slender fingers and toes were not made for striding or digging in the sand.

I thought about *deserts* and shuddered to myself.

Leaning slightly forward, my new master took up the ladle, dipped it into the bowl and poured the contents over his head, eyes closed as water streamed over his bare head and coursed down his face. A profound look of peace settled over his features, and I hated him a little bit for it.

Once, twice...well, I trust you can count. Let me say that one hundred ablutions performed with Shaladan deliberation takes a fair bit of time.

And this was only the first ritual of the first day of the rest of my spirits-forsaken life.

When Farad Dhoul finished, he replaced the ladle on its stand, rewound his turban around his head, and went about his business. I rose from my kneeling-mat, picked up the empty bowl, balanced it on my shaved head, and went about mine.

This time, the strangeness of it all struck me as it hadn't on my first foray. The city was awake and bustling, and I had to thread my way through a crowd in the marketplace. No one would meet my eyes. Of course not—ordinary Keren weren't permitted to address the handmaids. I knew that. I'd grown up knowing it. Mistress Elia had reminded us of it daily. And yet I hadn't had the first inkling of how it would make me feel, at once horribly conspicuous and utterly invisible.

Even my own *Ma* looked away when I passed, cuffing my little brother Joji when he pointed and called out to me in an excited voice.

And I had to look away from him as though I hadn't heard, tears trickling from my eyes, lest one of Mistress Elia's spies among the older handmaids, the ones who had nothing left to live for but duty and status and zealously guarded our honor, report me for acknowledging a Keren commoner. Some of the younger handmaids, those with a spark of liveliness left in them, had warned us initiates, never trust anyone with ten strands or more.

When I reached the river, Shoni was among the handmaids in the ford, stepping carefully across the flat rocks, her bowl balanced on her head. It had only been a day, but I'd never been so glad to see anyone in my life.

I waited until she reached the shore safely to acknowledge her. "Greetings, sister. Are you well?"

"I am." The mutinous look in her eyes said otherwise. "And you?"

Glancing around for spies, I lowered my voice. "Oh, Shoni! I don't know if I can bear this."

Shoni freed one hand to give me a quick, surreptitious pinch. "You can!" she hissed. "Be strong!"

I did my best.

I filled my bowl and returned to my master's household, ringing the bell to summon his wife, my mistress Alaya. She, too, welcomed me to Shakrath's service before performing the ritual of a hundred ablutions. I fetched a bowl for Atika, the elder daughter, who did not deign to greet me. When she had finished, I went back to the river and fetched a bowl for Amina, the younger daughter, who performed the ritual carefully under the watchful eye of their governess. And at last, in the waning hours of the afternoon, I hurried to fetch a bowl for the governess Resalin before the gates of the city were locked at sundown.

By the end of the day, my head and neck and feet ached, and I was so exhausted, I could barely pick at the food the silent Keren servant brought me. I fell onto my pallet and slept like the dead.

The next day, I did it again.

And the next, and the next, and the next, until the days began to blur into an endless stream.

Our only respite from our duties came once a month on the first day of the new moon, the day on which that poxy old desert chieftain was granted his vision three hundred years ago. On that day, the Shaladan rested and prayed, and the handmaids were permitted to return to the temple that our heads might be freshly shaved. Spirits save me, to think that I'd dreaded the prospect when I left the temple! Youthful vanity be damned—three days into my service, and the first new moon couldn't come fast enough for me. For the space of a blessed hour or two while we waited our turn in line, we were able to converse with relative freedom, so long as we didn't speak ill of our service. Shoni was particularly adept at making sure she and I were near the end of the line.

Were it not for new moon days, I think I would have lost my wits in the years that followed.

Let me be clear—and I *do* wish to be clear in light of what happened—no one in Farad Dhoul's household was unkind to me. Not by Shaladan standards, which do not reckon forcing me into a life of service to a god I came to resent with every fiber of my being to be a cruelty.

No, I was fed well and lodged like a member of the household. As I grew hardened to the labor and able to more swiftly accomplish the task of fetching five bowls of water from the river over the course of a day, the governess Resalin encouraged me to listen to the girls' afternoon lessons that I might enhance my understanding of Shaladan history and the worship of Shakrath. Although I could scarce have cared less about either, it passed the time. I learned to speak in a manner befitting my unwanted status. I conceived a certain fondness for Amina, the younger daughter. At eight years of age when my service began, she was only a few inches taller than me, too young yet for head-scarves and earrings. Having only ever known my elderly predecessor, Amina was inclined to treat me as an interesting new playmate.

After his initial greeting, Farad Dhoul himself seldom spoke to me. My mistress Alaya had cause to reprimand me for minor breaches of etiquette on occasion—not many, mind you, for I had an abiding fear of being banished to the desert—but she did it without rancor. Only once was she obliged to order me to fast for the day in punishment, and afterward, she gave me one of her nicer not-terribly-worn head-scarves so that I might know that she bore me no grudge for it. In four years, I never had to report to the temple for a whipping.

And yet I chafed.

Do you wish to know more about the Shaladan? Let me tell you, the Shaladan are *slow*. They have a saying: *Swift in battle, deliberate in all other matters*. Every thought uttered, every motion made, is slow; endlessly, agonizingly deliberate and *slow*. They can spend hours lost in contemplation of Shakrath's ineffable majesty, and they simply cannot comprehend that others cannot—or have no desire to do so.

There were times on the kneeling-mat, waiting for a member of the household to finish his or her ablutions, when I could have rent my robes and screamed and wept out of sheer frustration.

One hundred ablutions. I thought that until the day I died, I would never understand it.

The Keren are a *quick* folk; quick to laugh, quick to love, quick to anger, quick to forgive and forget. Beside the slow, ponderous grace of the Shaladan, we are as quick and darting as sparrows on the wing; and as fragile and short-lived, too.

Walking through the market with my bowl balanced atop my head, I could not help but be conscious of the quick blood beating in my veins, hot with desire and envy. Although I dared not acknowledge them, I saw boys I had known grow into young men with sinewy limbs and quick, ready smiles.

Any of them could have been mine.

One of them *should* have been mine.

By sixteen, I felt as ripe and bursting as a plum. My body was strong with labor, my skin was glossy with the health imparted by a rich diet. Beneath my blue robe, my breasts were full and high and firm. I yearned to be touched, stroked, held; I yearned to do the same in return.

In the silence of my own thoughts, I prayed to the myriad nameless spirits of field and stream.

Let me be free, I prayed; and then, daring more, *let* us *be free. Let the true sons and daughters of the Kerentari valley be free of our Shaladan masters.*

Although I cannot say for sure, I suspect the spirits were unaccustomed to being asked for great things. By and large, the prayers of the Keren people were as modest as our hopes and dreams. Living for centuries under Shaladan occupation, we had long ago accepted our roles as a simple given truth, something we could alter no more than we could the weather. And had I not been chosen as a handmaid, I daresay I would never have thought otherwise.

Oh, well; there was more to it, but that came later. All I knew at sixteen was that I wanted my freedom.

At eighteen, with five strands of finely-wrought silver around my neck, I began to gain a deeper understanding of all that the loss of that freedom entailed.

Children.

I'd mourned the loss of my family, the family into which I was born. I'd mourned the loss of the husband with whom I would never lie. But it wasn't until the day that I saw my older sister Juna in the market that I began to mourn the loss of the family of my own that I would never have. Juna had married a rope-maker's son, and she'd been entrusted to mind the family's spot in the marketplace for the first time that day. I stopped short and stared at the sight of her, two little boys tugging at the coarse undyed fabric of her skirts and a third babe at the breast. My sister glanced up absently, then stared back at me, open-mouthed in shock. As I stood there in my fine blue robes, my silver bowl balanced atop my shaved head, five strands of silver draped around my neck, I saw her look of shock give way to pity.

In that moment, I would have given anything to trade lives with her. I would have given a great deal just to *talk* to her, to meet my little nephews and the newest babe.

But no, even that small pleasure was forbidden to me. It was forbidden to us both. I watched Juna remember and look away, bowing her head over the small figure of the babe suckling at her breast.

My own breasts ached in sympathy and I felt a profound emptiness deep inside me. I would never know a man, never hold a babe in my arms. The household of Farad Dhoul would be all the family I would ever have. I would serve as a handmaid of Shakrath until I was too old and weak to complete my duties, and then retire to the temple and wait to die.

Oh, I had known all this, of course; but on that day I felt the knowledge of this settle into my flesh and bones.

"What's wrong, Dala?" Amina asked me later that day; little Amina, the closest thing I'd ever have to a child of my own, who now stood a full foot and a half taller than me. At twelve years of age, she'd recently donned the head-scarf and dangling earrings of a young lady. "You seem sad."

"It's nothing, young mistress." I made myself smile at her. "Only that I saw my sister in the market today, and it grieved me that I could not speak to her."

Amina blinked. "Oh, but surely…surely it is nothing to the honor of being chosen to serve Shakrath?"

"Surely you are right, young mistress," I murmured.

"Here." She worked a bracelet loose from her wrist and held it out to me. "Wear my bangle today! It will remind you of the gifts that Shakrath has showered upon you and cheer you."

I averted my head to hide my tears as I accepted the bangle. "Thank you, young mistress. You are too kind."

Amina smiled at the compliment. "You are very welcome, Dala. I do not want you to be sad."

After that day, I took a different route through the market to avoid seeing my sister and her little ones. It meant my journey to and from the river was a little longer, but no one in the household commented on it.

It was on the next new moon day that Shoni pulled me close to her as we waited in line at the temple to have our heads shaved, putting her lips against my ear as she used to do when we were initiates gossiping in bed; only it was something far more dangerous than gossip that she whispered to me. "When you go to the river tomorrow at dawn, make your way to the far bank, near the bamboo thicket, and wait for me to beckon to you."

Alarmed, I drew back from her. "Why?"

Shoni gave me a sharp pinch on the arm. "I'm trusting you with my life telling you this!" she said in a furious whisper. "Do you want to be a handmaid for the rest of your spirits-forsaken life?"

I shook my head.

"Then do it." She let go my arm.

I spent the rest of the day in an agony of suspense, torn between terror and excitement. What in the world could Shoni be thinking? A deliberate breach of etiquette—no, not even a breach of etiquette, but an abandonment of our duty—that severe would earn us both whippings for certain, maybe even the prospect of banishment. For Shoni, the latter was even likely. In the past four years, she'd been whipped more than once for carelessness that bordered on outright disobedience. I slept poorly, tossing and turning on my pallet, dreading the coming dawn.

By the time the bell rang, summoning me to my duty, I had half resolved to ignore Shoni; and yet I found my feet carrying me along my old, familiar route through the marketplace. Although the market wasn't open yet, the vendors were laying out their wares and I saw my sister among them, carefully arraying coils of rope on the dusty ground.

Did I take that route knowing that the sight of Juna and her little ones would goad my heart?

Or did I take it knowing that it would gain me a few spare minutes of time on my journey?

Both, maybe.

At the ford, there was a knot of handmaids in the center of the river, exchanging such pleasantries as were permitted to us during the execution of our duties. At first I thought they meant to block my path as I picked my way across the flat stones, taking care not to let the shallow rushing water dampen the hem of my robe. But no, they moved aside to let me pass, closing ranks behind me, and

I saw that none of them wore more than seven strands of silver around their necks.

On the far side of the river stood a thicket of bamboo, green and dense. “Hssst!” Shoni’s head poked out of a gap and she beckoned urgently to me. Carrying my bowl tucked under my right arm and holding up the skirts of my robe with my left hand, I went to her. “This way.” Catching my arm, she led me down a narrow pathway through the towering bamboo.

At the end of the path there was a small clearing, with several handmaids and a dozen men in it.

Men.

All Keren men, I thought at first, some of them from the northern slopes of the valley, taller and broader and lighter-skinned than us southerners. And then one of the tall ones lifted one arm and pointed at me with a fierce, hard grin, and I saw that his eyeteeth were curved and sharp and his eyes themselves… spirits save me, his eyes were green and his pupils were vertical like a cat’s.

No, not northern Keren.

Jagan.

They were conferring amongst themselves. The one who’d pointed at me was nodding. He hadn’t taken his gaze off me and I couldn’t look away from him, either. I’d never seen one of the Jagan before in my life, and yet it felt as though I knew him. My ears were filled with the sound of my own rushing blood, and then beneath it I heard a voice that sounded like a thousand voices at once whispering through the bamboo say, *now, now, the hour is upon us.*

My knees began to tremble and I dropped my bowl.

"Hush!" Shoni picked it up and thrust it at me. "Make no noise! It's worth our lives to get caught." She lowered her voice. "It's you, isn't it?"

I clutched my bowl tightly. "I don't understand."

He was picking his way across the clearing toward me. I stood as though rooted to the spot. "For three years now, our people have gone hungry," he said to me. "I prayed to the spirits of wind and stone, and I had a vision. *You* were in it."

I swallowed. "Oh?"

He pried one of my hands loose from my bowl and held it. His hand was warm and strong and callused. "Yes." His thumb rubbed over my skin, his green gaze intent upon mine. My pulse hammered in my veins, between my thighs. "You were holding our son. How are you called?"

"Dala," I whispered.

"Dala." He sighed my name softly, the sound like the breeze rustling through the bamboo thicket. "Dala, I am Valek. And we are meant to be together, you and I." Letting go of my hand, he turned to the others. "The spirits have spoken truly! The hour of shared destiny is upon us."

If Shoni hadn't caught my elbow to steady me, I might have fallen over. "I don't understand," I said again.

"I'm sorry." She gave my elbow a squeeze. "I was sworn to secrecy." Releasing me, she placed one hand on the shoulder of a grave-faced Keren man of middle years. "This is my Da," she said with pride. "All of you, listen fast and hard to what he has to say."

There was a plan, and it was simple and terrible.

Keren rebels armed with nothing more than kitchen knives and clubs stood not the slightest chance of rising up against our Shaladan masters without Jagan aid. The Jagan fighters were few in number and stood not the slightest chance of taking the city or prevailing over the many powerful Shaladan without Keren aid.

Therefore, in the darkest depths of the next new moon night, Keren rebels would unlock the city gates to admit a Jagan raiding party.

The handmaids in league with the rebellion would unlock the doors of their Shaladan households. And the Shaladan, taken by surprise in their sleep by an enemy who could see in the dark, would be slaughtered.

Afterward, the Keren and the Jagan would share ownership of the Kerentari valley in equal measure.

"It will be so." The Jagan clan-leader Valek touched my face. "I have seen it, Dala." There was a yearning tenderness in his voice. "No more will our mothers and sisters in the mountains starve during years of drought and blight. No more will our Keren brothers and sisters slave for the Shaladan and live on their leavings."

All I could think about was the amount of innocent blood that would be shed. "Surely you don't mean to—"

Shoni glanced at the sky and started in alarm at the lateness of the hour, grabbing my arm again. "Handmaids, quick! We dare stay no longer."

The enormity and daring and, yes, awfulness of the conspiracy was almost too much to ponder. I moved through the remainder of the day as though in a waking dream. Farad Dhoul reprimanded me for dawdling, his tone grave and disappointed, and I nodded in blank acceptance. I made four more trips to the river, my feet finding the way of their own accord. I passed my sister Juna's spot in the marketplace without seeing her or her little ones.

I remember only that Shoni approached me at the ford on my last journey to the river. "Tomorrow at dawn," she murmured, after a quick glance around. "Same place. Valek wishes to see you alone."

"Alone?" I echoed. She gave me a significant look, and I flushed in sudden understanding. "Oh."

She raised her eyebrows at me. "Will you be there?"

A handmaid with at least twelve strands frowned in our direction. "I don't know," I said and fled, water slopping over the sides of my bowl—a breach of etiquette that was reported before sundown.

I went to bed hungry and dazed that night.

How many times had I prayed that the spirits might grant freedom to me and my people? Many, many times. And yet I had never reckoned that it might come at such a terrible cost.

I prayed for guidance and received none.

I prayed for wisdom and found none.

Valek.

His face swam before me, high-boned and lean beneath a thick shock of black hair. Like the Shaladan chieftain centuries ago, he'd had a vision. The lush Kerentari valley, it seemed, inspired visions. Only this time, I was at the heart of one.

In the morning, I went to him. Once again, the handmaids conspired to block me from view that I might slip through the gap in the bamboo grove and find my way to the clearing.

He was waiting for me. No one else was present.

"I don't…" My voice sounded faint and weak and uncertain. "I'm sorry. I don't know."

"Dala." He beckoned to me. "Come."

I stayed where I was.

Valek laughed and approached me instead. "Set down the symbol of your servitude." He took the bowl from my unresisting grasp and placed it on the ground. "What is it you do not know?"

"You," I whispered.

"But you do know me." He cupped my face in his hands, and his breath was warm against my skin. "I have *seen* it, Dala. You and I are the stone on which our people will found our lives together." He stroked my lips with his thumb, slow and lingering. "Will you tell me you do not feel it, too? How can you believe otherwise?"

I grasped his wrists. "I don't—"

He kissed me.

It was not a tentative, gentle kiss such as I remembered granting my young Keren suitors when I was fourteen and no one's handmaid. It was a *man's* kiss, make no mistake about it, and I groaned and clutched his wrists as his tongue thrust boldly into my mouth, unleashing four years' worth of pent-up desire.

Lifting his head, Valek laughed softly, his cat-slitted eyes gleaming. "Ah! You *do* know."

"Hush!" Fierce with need, I breathed the word. My hands found his shoulder blades and pulled him closer.

Fierce.

It was an apt word for our coupling; short, sharp and fierce. It was as though a great storm rolled over the Kerentari valley and swept us up in its wake. There was no love in it—how could there have been? His vision notwithstanding, we were strangers to one another. And yet he was right, there was something in me that knew him, that understood that there was power in this joining. It hurt when he pushed into me the first time, but it was a pain I welcomed, a pain that tasted of freedom and defiance. We were not just man and woman, cock and cunny, but mountain and valley, rebel and ally. It was an act of desire and insurrection.

Afterward, I knew fear again.

"I must go," I said. "Only tell me…tell me you don't mean to put Shaladan women and children to the sword?"

"It is not our wish to do so. But they will resist, and nothing is certain in the dark, even for us." Valek fished a bulging leather pouch from his rucksack and pressed it into my palm, folding my fingers over it. "Khes-flower ointment. Mark the door of your household and yourself with it." He mimed dipping his thumb into it and smearing it over his brow. "It will shine in the dark to Jagan eyes. You must share it with the other handmaids."

I tucked the greasy pouch into the sleeve of my robe, retrieved my silver bowl, and hurried back to my duties.

Throughout the day, I could not help but be acutely aware of what I'd done. There was the lingering soreness and an echo of unfamiliar pleasure. Valek's seed mingled with traces of my virginal blood trickled down my inner thighs.

When I took my place on the kneeling-pad and waited for Farad Dhoul to complete his ritual, it seemed to me that surely he would know, that he would sense the difference in me and denounce me as unclean, no longer fit to serve as a handmaid of

Shakrath, fit only for banishment to the desert where I would die of thirst beneath the merciless sun and the wind and sand would strip the flesh from my bones.

But no, I was wrong. So long as I carried out my duty with no breach of etiquette, my master noticed nothing. Almighty Shakrath, whose honor demanded he be served only by virgin maids, breathed no hint of my transgression in his ear. So long as I obeyed, I was just another implement in the ritual.

It made me angry, and anger made me careless. I managed to constrain it before the master and mistress of the household, but I slammed the elder daughter Atika's bowl in the tripod hard enough to spill water. Although Atika didn't witness it, she caught me in the act of trying to mop the spill with my robes.

If it had been little Amina, she might have covered for my breach, but Atika had a haughty streak that reckoned any error was a personal affront. My mistress Alaya regretted sending me to the temple for a whipping, but she sent me nonetheless.

I bore it and seethed.

Now that there was a possibility that the order of the world I'd taken for granted my whole life might well and truly be overturned, I saw the manifest injustice of it everywhere; in the fields and orchards where the Keren labored from sunrise to sunset; in the hovels along the city walls where poor Keren clustered in crowded, filthy quarters; in the markets where the Keren bartered for grubs while the Shaladan pondered fattened livestock at their leisure; in Farad Dhoul's household where Keren servants saw to their masters' every need. Why should the Keren spend their lives in toil and squalor so that the Shaladan might spend theirs contemplating the majesty of Shakrath in luxury? Well, I'll tell you why: For no good reason but that it pleases the Shaladan.

Maybe it pleases Shakrath, too—but I wasn't so impressed with the all-knowing, all-wise Shakrath anymore.

No, not since I'd known what it was to lie with a man, and found my master all unwitting of the fact that I was in violation of Shakrath's sacred law.

After that day, Valek did not send for me again, but it didn't matter. What was needful to fulfill our destiny had been done. The conspiracy continued apace. Young handmaids at the ford exchanged knowing glances. My lacerated back stung as I went about my duties, the sweat-soaked cloth of my fine blue robe clinging to the welts Mistress Elia's whip had raised. I filled a twist of oilcloth with khes-flower ointment, hid it in my chamber, and passed the leather pouch on to Shoni at the ford with quick muttered instructions.

She nodded, the pouch vanishing into her sleeve. "I'll see that it's done."

"Shoni." I hesitated, then asked her a question that had been plaguing me. "Why did you wait so long to approach me?"

She smiled, but there was bitterness in it. "I knew about Valek's vision. I suppose I was hoping it wouldn't be you, Dala. I knew I would envy whoever was chosen."

"Don't," I murmured. "Please don't. I would trade places with you if I could."

Shoni shrugged as though she didn't care and hoisted her brimming silver bowl in a practiced motion. She balanced it atop her head, and walked away from me, her back swaying gracefully.

I have wondered so many times—was there something I should have done differently? Something I *could* have done differently? Perhaps; and yet I can think of no course of action that would not have resulted in my banishment to the desert and a lingering death to follow, for as the new moon swelled to full, my woman's courses failed to arrive, and I knew the seed that Valek had planted in me, the seed that was meant to join our peoples, had taken root.

I was with child, and if I were found out, it would be the death of us. And so I kept my silence.

All too soon, the next new moon day was upon us.

For the first time, I dreaded the day that had been my sole respite. I didn't trust myself to speak to Shoni or any of the other handmaids in the conspiracy, but took a spot in line as quickly as I could that I might be done with it. I found myself shuddering at the touch of Mistress Elia's keen blade scraping over my stubbly scalp, causing her to nick me. She swatted me in annoyance, gave me a rag to stanch the bleeding, finished the job and sent me on my way.

I daubed khes-flower ointment on the door of Farad Dhoul's household and went inside to wait for nightfall.

It was the longest wait of my life.

At sunset, the other Keren servants were sent to their separate quarters and the great front door was locked from within. I smeared khes-flower ointment on my brow. There was a trace of ointment left in the twist of oil-cloth. I hesitated, then left my chamber to intercept Amina and Atika in the hallway outside the chamber they shared.

"Dala!" Amina's long, lashless eyes widened in surprise at my breach of etiquette. "Should you not be abed?"

"Forgive me, young mistress," I said humbly. "I had a cramp in my foot and needed to walk."

Atika's eyes narrowed with disapproval. "You should have walked in your chamber. We'll have to tell Mother in the morning."

"Yes, mistress," I said to her, then reached up to brush my ointment-smeared thumb over Amina's brow. "Forgive me, young mistress," I said again. "There was a fly."

As I returned to my chamber, I could hear them discussing the incident in slow, puzzled murmurs, but soon enough the household was quiet, all its members sunk deep in slumber. I stole forth from my chamber one last time, making my way by touch, to unlock the great door from within.

For a moment, I considered fleeing—but it was already too late. If the rebellion failed, I would be caught and banished. If the rebellion succeeded, I would be thought to have betrayed it.

I made my way back to my chamber and waited alone in the darkness until the raid.

Thus it came to pass that on the first night of the new moon, my master Farad Dhoul was slain in his sleep. His wife Alaya took up his sword and fought until she was slain. The governess Resalin heard the commotion and rushed to the girls' defense. She was killed fighting tooth and nail in their chamber. Atika sustained grave wounds and was taken captive. She died of her injuries before the night was out. Only little Amina, with a smudge of khes-flower ointment shining on her brow, was spared. She was taken captive, too.

I know, because I heard the tales later.

But that night, I sat as rigid and unmoving as a stone on my pallet, one hand splayed over my belly while the terrible sounds of the raid in progress—the clashing of swords, the cries of pain and fury—echoed in my ears and tore at my heart. Once, the door to my chamber was opened by a pair of Jagan raiders. They glanced at me, flashed hard smiles and victorious hand-signs, and closed the door.

The household grew quiet once more.

I continued to sit motionless.

Valek found me at dawn, wrenching open my chamber door. He was splashed head to foot with blood, but he was grinning fiercely. A handful of Jagan raiders and Keren rebels accompanied him, the latter armed with swords taken from dead Shaladan warriors that made them look like little boys at play with their fathers' weapons. "There you are!" Valek strode into the chamber, his cat-slitted eyes glittering with triumph. "Come, Dala! The city is ours." He held out one blood-stained hand to me. "Let our people see us together and rejoice!"

"Excuse me." I rose from my pallet, picked up my silver bowl and balanced it atop my head. "I have a duty to perform."

He reached for my arm to stop me.

"No," one of the Keren said, and the others nodded. "Let her go."

No one disturbed me as I walked through the city. Here and there, there were still knots of fighting; besieged and isolated Shaladan households whose handmaids hadn't joined the conspiracy holding out against their attackers. Not enough to turn the tide, though. Valek was right, we'd taken the city.

There were Shaladan dead in the streets, corpses dragged from their homes and piled like cordwood. In the marketplace, the few Shaladan women and children who'd been spared and taken captive were confined under heavy guard in a pen that usually held sheep or goats. I didn't know what plans the rebels had in store for them. Later, I would learn if whatever influence I wielded might aid them in their plight, but I could do nothing for them now.

"Dala!" Amina called out to me in anguish as I passed. "Dala, *please*! Help me!"

Feeling as though my heart was breaking in my chest, I ignored her.

At the ford, I gathered the skirts of my fine blue robe, taking care not to let them trail in the water.

I filled my silver bowl.

Balancing it atop my freshly shaved head, I made my way back through the city and returned to the household of Farad Dhoul with its blood-spattered walls. On the sun terrace, I placed the bowl in the tripod, careful not to spill a drop.

There was no need to strike the gilded bell with the hammer. There was no one to summon but me. There was no one to make atonement but me. I took the silver ladle from its carved wooden rest and dipped it into the bowl.

Pouring water over my head, I began counting.